The Locket

Isabelle Call

AOS Publishing, 2023

ISBN: 978-1-990496-23-3

Cover Design: Chanelle Poupart

Visit AOS Publishing's website:
www.aospublishing.com

Part One

Chapter 1

an uneasiness

Shelly

Shelly had always thought that, maybe, she was just crazy. That the things that went bump in the night were exactly what her parents had said they were; a shifting of the building, her cat scratching at her bed or laying across her face as she slept. Cats sometimes did that they would say, they had no regard for personal space and so they would curl up on your face while you slept. Even so, if it was her cat she couldn't help but recoil at the thought of her blessed minx doing that to her. Suffocating in her sleep had always been one of her fears, she even braided her hair back before bed to avoid the possibilities of it knotting itself around her neck. And a shifting building, well that made her nervous too, how sturdy could a house be if every night it had to resettle itself, crack and wriggle its bones into comfortability so it didn't come crashing down on them. No, her parents words of reassurance didn't really reassure her at all.

"You're paranoid sweet heart, that's all. We've lived here for years. Longer than youd be able to remember. If there was something here I would know," she had memorized her mothers bed time speech to her.

This speech had started after Shelly had asked her mother if schizophrenia ran in her family. She had read somewhere that it was genetic, so if others had it she probably did to. Her mother had looked at her pointedly and then let out a soft chuckle before beginning her speech. And from that night onward, Shelly heard it almost every time she mentioned a corner of the house that seemed a bit too dark, or a noise in her ear that sounded a bit too human.

She supposed she was right though, her mother would know if something were here. After all, her mother had always told her she could see the dead. It wasn't in a spooky way, not really, it was in more of the way that everyone else saw the living. That's how her mom had explained it to her. There were people who would walk down the street next to everyone else but something about them just seemed different. She wasn't sure exactly what that difference was but she knew it was there and she knew they were dead. This wasn't always the case, the difference was still there but sometimes she would see someone in what looked like a 1920's flapper dress or in a worn through cowboy outfit with a bullet hole going right through them. Those people she knew were dead before noticing that the differences were there. She would tell Shelly that she didn't need to worry because ghosts couldn't hurt her, they hardly even interacted with the living at all. At most, all a ghost could do was give you the heebie jeebies.

▪

"Is that what you feel Shelly? Just a sense of the heebie jeebies?" Her mother had asked her this one night when Shelly was feeling particularly uneasy.

She had been starring out her window as the rain pattered down and blurred the lights of the city that surrounded their apartment. Vancouver, the rainy city, everyone thought that was Seattle but she thought that's just because everyone seemed to forget about Canada. The American's ran the show and no one cared about her city just North of the border, heck, everyone's favourite movies were all filmed here and no one even knew it. Oh well, she would think to herself as she stared out into the gloom, I know this is the real rainy city and that's what matters, I know it and the ghosts know it too. This night, she had starred out into the street and saw a man with his chin tucked close to his chest scurrying along with a newspaper held tightly to his head. He stood out against the dark greys of the rain-covered buildings with his bright blue jacket as it reflected the colours of the street lights back to her. She watched him for a while as he weaved in and out of the crowds of people who all seemed to be dressed in black. And then suddenly, he just stopped. He stopped and turned around and looked right at her, only for a moment, but she knew it had been her that he was looking at.

No, it wasn't the heebie jeebies that Shelly had felt that night it was something else. The man, she had thought, had looked at her with what seemed to be pity. It was that pity, that look of sadness in his eyes as they met hers which had made her so uneasy that night. It wasn't the heebie jeebies, but it was something, and it was a something she felt again three years later when her parents told her they were going to move.

Chapter 2

something

3 years later

The something crept up into Shelly's throat the way acid did when you were sick and your stomach decided now might be a good time to eject all of its contents. She took a deep breath and swallowed, hoping for it to go away, it didn't.

"Isn't that exciting hun?" Her mom was all full of joy and nearly jumping out of her shoes with glee.

She had just returned from what Shelly had assumed was some kind ofwork meeting but was now learning was actually a meeting with a realtor that her parents had been seeing for the past few months without her. So this is what it's like to be cheated on, no wonder women kill their husbands, she had thought as her mother told her the news.

"Come on Shelly belly," an annoying knick name she had gotten at the age of four when her parents captured a half naked picture of her with a melted fudgesicle stick in her right hand, and the previous contents of that stick on her tummy that had unfortunately stuck. A nickname that no 20 year old girl wanted to have. "It's gonna be great, we're finally gonna have the space to get that dog we've always talked about."

Shelly and her dad had talked about getting a dog since she saw her first horror movie, a frightening thing called I am Legend; a zombie flick starring the true love of her mothers life, Will Smith. She had watched it in a themed jail house bunk bed in West Edmonton Mall on a small family vacation. She had been eight so her parents agreed that she was finally allowed to watch a scary movie, Will's face had been plastered across every screen and billboard for the three months leading up to the trip, so his movie had seemed like the obvious choice. What she hadn't expected was to see a movie that was so frightening she wouldn't be able to sleep for the next two weeks, a movie she still couldn't watch. Her boyfriend, now ex, had always made fun of her for that.

He would poke her in the side when they sat down and flicked on Netflix, "come onnn," he would prod, "it's not even scary, you're just being a wimp."

Maybe she was being a wimp but that little eight-year-old girl still had a tight hold on that memory and had loaded it with fear. She would never watch that movie again. The only thing she liked about it, aside from the adrenaline rush, was Will's dog. He had been loyal until the end, and she loved that about dogs. Her dad loved that too. But getting a dog in a downtown Vancouver apartment wasn't the ideal situation. Her dad always said they needed space to run, to be free, and to just be a dog; the city was not this place.

"I knew you'd like that, come on, who doesn't want to live on an island." Shelly's dad pinched her cheek and gave his hand a little shake, he seemed to forget she was twenty, not six.

But a smile had made its way to the corners of her mouth and he was right, she had liked the idea of getting a dog, not enough to be happy at the thought of moving though, and soon the smile faded.

Her mom frowned as she saw the blank expression return to Shelly's face, "come on hun, we can finally afford to buy a house. This is very exciting news," she annunciated the words *very exciting news*, taking long breaks in between each one, as though Shelly were still a toddler, "it's not even that far away, just a quick ferry ride. You'll be able to come back to the city and see your friends all the time. They can even come stay with us on weekends, and reading breaks!"

"Mom, I just-," Shelly trailed off and slumped into the old tattered couch which seemed to be the backdrop in all of her baby photos, "what if I can't make any friends?"

"You will hun, I promise," her mom moved behind her, gently wrapping her arms around Shelly's shoulder and kissing the top of her head, "it's going to be a great fresh start. Plus, being in nature might help to lessen your anxiety a little."

Shelly doubted it.

▪

She crawled into bed that night with her laptop, opening it to her google search and typing in dogs for adoption. She had never really been one for buying a perfectly bred dog from a breeder and spending thousands, a shelter dog was the way for her to go. This she knew her father would completely agree with her on, after all her grandparents had taken him in.

▪

Shelly's father was found in the same way that all good adoption stories start, wrapped up in a blanket and placed in a box on the steps of a church. The only difference being that he was in a carrier, a decently expensive one, but the classic story of the blanket stayed the same. He had been about one and a half when he was left there. Too young to remember anything of his birth parents the social worker had said had said, but he swore he remembered the smell of his birth mothers perfume. Sometimes he would stop dead in his tracks when they walked through Nordstrom and an old woman walked by, swearing she smelled just like her. He would turn with her as she walked by and study her, as if matching his features to hers, trying to find a resemblance. A couple times he did find some, the colouring of their hair and their eyes, the long straight vertical of their noses, even the way that they walked, but he never called out. He would always just sigh and turn back around to continue their aimless walking through the high end department store where they never actually bought anything. Her dad had told her he liked to take her there because he felt it helped to push her to choose a good career, one that made her happy and also allowed her to shop where all the fancy women shopped.

Shelly felt differently, she thought he took her there because he hoped that one day he might run into the woman who left him in that carrier, in such a cliché, but never the less she enjoyed their time together looking at the shoes and the bags that they weren't able to afford.

Not that they were broke either, her parents both had good jobs, her dad was the manager of a hotel in the famous Gastown, and her mom worked at a local tattoo shop; she hoped that when they moved she could start up her own shop, and her husband would be able to pursue his dream of being a graphic novelist. Her parents had met in art school, young and full of ambition to be world renowned artists in their fields. Life had other plans though, when her dad started his internship as an illustrator her mom had just found out she was pregnant, so he stepped up and left behind his dream to work at the hotel. Shelly always felt guilty for that, she knew it wasn't her fault and that her dad loved working at the hotel, but they had always pushed her to follow her dreams and she wished he was able to do the same. So they weren't broke, they were just an average family who were able to afford an apartment in downtown Vancouver because her grandparents had bought it as an investment property in 1976.

-

She thought about her parents as her screen loaded, maybe this move wasn't such a bad thing. If her parents could do what they loved and feel more financially secure, what was so bad about that?

As the screen finally loaded with what seemed like an endless row of search results for dogs for adoption Shelly set to work, noting that the something in her throat had begun to disappear.

Los Angeles

Mexico

Texas

Ontario

"Jeez, where're all the shelters near me," she said aloud to her screen as she clicked on one of the dogs with the location Texas listed beside it.

He was a beautiful dog, five months old and already a giant. From the picture, it looked like he would be close to the height of Shelly's knee, at only five months there was still a lot of growing left to do. She kept reading, a Great Pyrenees and Rottweiler mix, that explained the Rottweiler markings on such a fluffy dog, his name was listed as Edward. He was up to date on all of his shots, neutered, and even knew some commands. Those listed were; come here, sit down, roll over, and stay. She moved her cursor to the top of the web page and hit the "send" button, she typed in dad then hit enter. She scrolled through a few more listings, there was a gold retriever in Washington, a mix of who knew what that was kind of cute in Ontario, a Chihuahua in Los Angeles, but none of them called to her in the way that Edward had.

She figured she had probably searched enough for the night and that the bed was calling to her now too. She closed her computer and placed it on the stand next to her bed, shutting off the lamp that was illuminating her room as she did so. Soon she closed her eyes, and drifted off into the darkness.

▪

She dreamt often, sometimes of the ghosts her mother had described to her when she was younger, she still told her about the ghosts she saw, but usually it was in real time when they walked passed an old building or the grave yard. Ghosts were drawn to old things her mother told her, that's why she saw even the newer ghosts in the old places. She didn't know exactly how she knew that, she said it was like knowing that the ghosts had a difference, you didn't know exactly what it was you just knew it was there. Shelly couldn't see them like her mother could, but she could feel them, and often that feeling was strongest when her mother would suddenly stop and describe one that piqued her interest.

Still, to Shelly, the most interesting had been the old cowboy her mother had told her about when she was a kid, the one that had the bullet hole that went right through the middle of his body. She dreamt about him often, and tonight she did the same. His hat was low on his brow, as it always was, and the smoke from his cigar escaped the hole in his chest in little puffs. Beside him was Edward, standing at his full height of what looked like two and a half feet tall. Shelly was barely over five feet and Edward looked to be close to half her height, so she felt confident in her guess of his size. Edward's being there was new, but the cowboy was still the same. He had brown hair, the same colour as hers. It was braided down his back and an eagle feather had been braided into it and now stuck out the bottom of his hat. His hat was a beautiful tanned colour and had a beaded pattern of yellow, blues and reds wrapped around it.

Edward ran to her and nuzzled into her hip as the cowboy dismounted his horse. She frowned as she realized the dream was the same as it always was, just with Edward next to her this time. The cowboy pulled his cigar from his mouth and threw it to the ground. He picked up his boot as he always did, putting it back down on the cigar as Shelly moved her head to mimic the motion. Right on cue. He ground his toe into the dirt beneath him, following this with a step toward Shelly, causing his spur to let out a bell like ring. She stepped forward before he could lift his arm to motion her closer, knowing what was going to happen. As she moved closer the cowboy lifted his hand to his head tilting his hat upwards to reveal a weathered face tinted gold by the sun and piercing green eyes. His eyes were sad as he looked at her, and she was reminded of the man in the blue rain jacket she had seen on the street years ago.

"I'm sorry," was all he said, and just as quickly he was on his horse and heading away from her into the desert.

This was when she usually woke up, but not this time. A puzzled look found its way to her brow and she looked down at Edward, who tilted his head to the side in response. She let out a sigh to calm herself down and did a slow three-hundred-and-sixty-degree turn. She had never looked behind her. She had always just assumed there was a town back there like the ones in the old western movies her grandpa used to watch, but there wasn't. All there was behind her was only more desert. When she turned back around again to where her cowboy had been she noticed that behind her hadn't just been more desert, it had been a mirror. The same plateaus that jutted up from the orange sand in front of her were exactly the same as the ones behind her only they were backwards. The cactuses were the same too. She took a half staggering step back and looked up at the sky. The clouds cut themselves perfectly down the middle above her head to mimic the ones to the front of her. How had she never looked up? As the thought crossed her mind Edward let out a low growl and stepped carefully behind her. She turned slowly, not expecting to see anything because there was nothing to see in front of her. However, there was something to see, a pack of coyotes was staring back at her from the open plain. Where had they come from? And why weren't they mirrored? The pack leapt forward, yipping. Suddenly it sounded as though she was surrounded on all sides. Whipping back around Shelly saw that she was wrong. She did not think to turn back to see them advancing as her own dogs growl grew louder, instead she decided the best thing she could do was run.

She ran as quickly as she could, only glancing over her shoulder once as the yipping grew louder, to see a her Edward fighting off three of the pack while the other two pursued her. She wanted to turn back for him but she knew she needed to keep going.

"Keep running, you just need to wake up. Wake up Shelly," she breathed to herself, half choking on the words as they tried to escape her dry throat.

She could no longer hear Edward and the three coyotes behind her, but she could hear the yips of her pursuers and they were getting closer. It sounded like they were laughing at her, as they gained. She felt the incisors of one brush against her Achilles and pushed forward, begging her legs to let her pick up the pace. No use, another graze, this time leaving a thin scrape. Tears began to rush down her cheeks as her legs started too slow. Wake up she thought, WAKE UP! Another tooth caught her, drawing blood. She saw a member of the pack gaining to her right, starting to try and circle. She could still hear her original two pursuers behind her. Edward, her heart sunk as she felt a set of jaws clamp down around her ankle. She fell forward, her arms outstretched.

Chapter 3

a sickness

Shelly woke up in a cold sweet, pulling her comforter up to her chin as her eyes slowly adjusted to the dark of her room. She let out a sigh of relief and then noticed something. Her ankle was sore, practically throbbing, as though she had been stuck by a row of sharp needles. Her fear settled back in and her stomach suddenly became so heavy she thought she might never be able to leave her bed; even so she tossed her blankets to the side and threw herself forwards and out of her bed. Her hand found the light switch after a couple panicked swipes at the wall and she quickly flipped the switch to the ceiling. Blinking rapidly to get her eyes to adjust to the light she steadied herself against the wall from the sudden rush she felt hitting her head. She took a deep breath and bent to look at her ankle, clear. There were no marks and no bruises, not even so much as a scrape. She stayed bent forwards for a minute, running her fingers over the spot where the pain had been, half hoping to feel raised skin that her eyes weren't able to find. There was nothing there.

Shelly crawled back into bed, this time leaving the lights on. She starred up at the '90's popcorn ceiling probably filled with asbestos, and rubbed at her ankle with her left heel. She knew she had felt the pain, knew it was real.

-

By the time the morning had rolled around and the shimmer of the dust as it spun in the air, illuminated by the beams of light peaking through her blinds had captured her attention, Shelly had convinced herself that she was being paranoid. Just as she always was. It had been a bad dream and nothing more, she had felt the pain so clearly because her mind was still in dream mode. She recalled an article she had read somewhere, or maybe it was a video she had watched on her instagram or something, it was a psychologist. The psychologist was talking about a study they had done about how our brains sometimes wake up after our body does, in the opposite way to sleep paralysis, we experience our reality physically while our brains and our nervous system are still in our dreams. That was most likely exactly what had happened last night. She had woken up physically when she had fallen in her dream, you couldn't die in your dreams, everyone knew that, so the threat of dying had woken her up. Then, because she had woken up so abruptly her brain wasn't able to keep up and it tricked her into thinking that the pain it believed it felt because of her dream was actually real. It was silly to read too much into explainable events, that was a speech her dad used to give her when her mom wasn't there to give hers.

"Shelly, everything is explainable, well, most things are explainable. And if you stop for a second to breath and allow yourself to look at something from a rational perspective, you'll see that it's silly to read too much into explainable events."

He was like that, her dad, always being rational. He didn't believe that her mom could see ghosts. He thought that she just had an over active imagination, and that when she saw little glimpses of something out of the corner of her eye she liked to make up stories to go along with them. Shelly might have agreed with her dad if it weren't for the feelings that would well up in her, a sense some might say, that some other being was with her. It wasn't quite the feeling of being watched but it was close. It was like that feeling you got when you were asleep on the couch as a kid and out of no where you could feel your parents come into the room, and so you started to pretend to be asleep even though you already were, so that they would carry you to bed.

This feeling of knowing was what had sold her on her moms stories and strayed her in the direction opposite her dads beliefs. That, and the fact that his belief system didn't always hold up. Nearly ten years prior to the dreaded conversation of the move they had been visiting her fathers parents at their family farm nearly seven hours north of the lower mainland. She never remembered the name of the town because she didn't care to, the air there felt stale and every time they crossed through the border crossing she had felt the need to make sure her window was rolled all the way up and that her door was locked.

▪

Her grandparents weren't farmers but her grandmothers mother had been, and she had grown up on the farm. She moved to Vancouver in her 20's to get away from the small rural life and pursue a life of academia, leaving her elder brother behind to run the place with his wife. Her name had been Shelly as well, Cecilia actually, but she had gone by Shelly for short. It was in Vancouver that she had met her husband, Shelly's great-grandfather, Andrei. He was a Romani man who had recently emigrated to Canada to begin his new position as a partner in a start-up law firm. Cecilia had been studying law at the time, and his partners secretary. She was a stalky woman, the farm girl couldn't fully be taken from her. She had thick, long black hair that ran the entire length of her back. Her features were strong and prominent, and she would often tell Shelly that it was her Chilcotin ancestors refusing to be forgotten. Her grandfather used to tell her stories of the first time he saw her; how he thought she was the strongest woman he had ever seen, she was beautiful to, he would always remind her, but he made a point to mention her presence, and how no matter what position she held in the firm she could still command the room. Andrei was a broad shouldered man and had warm olive skin. His smile showed a slightly crooked canine on the left side and scrunched up his eyes when it was wide, which was almost always, and Shelly had always thought he had very kind eyes when shown pictures of him . It was that cheeriness her grandmother would say when she spoke of him, that made her great grandmother fall for him. "Because a kind man is the best man" her grandma used to say to her and she would quickly tap her finger onto Shelly's nose as she said it.

-

Their romance took four years to form and eventually blossom into anything substantial, and by the time it had they were both so antsy they got married within two months. Within the year Cecilia had finished her degree and soon after Andrei left his partnership and he and Cecilia opened their own firm. Their marriage had been unconventional for the time to say the least, they had waited five years after marriage to have children, focusing heavily on their careers and Cecilia's completion of law school. When they eventually did have their first child, Andreea, Shelly's grandmother, they both continued with their work. They had decided on a plan to maintain their work and family lives, with Cecilia taking two months off to be with the baby, and Andrei the following two. They continued this pattern until Andreea began her education and Cecilia fell pregnant again. The pregnancy was plagued with sicknesses which Cecilia often attributed to the tall black figure that hunched itself up in the corner of her room, staring down at her from the ceiling. Of course, when Andrei looked there was nothing there, sometimes a slight shadow, but nothing more. Cecilia insisted and had told her husband that she was sure it was something that belonged to the house. Even in his reluctance to believe Cecilia about the creature which was draining her life force he agreed to move and soon they had moved to a house overlooking the water in West Vancouver. As Andrei had suspected the move did nothing to improve her health and he and Cecilia made their choice to have a late-term abortion, a choice highly criticized in that time and performed by few doctors. Following Cecilia's recovery was another illness. North, at their family home, her brother had contracted a severe case of measles, within a month he had died. He had left behind two daughters, neither of which he had any relationship with and so left the farm to his only other living relative, his sister. She in turn left the farm to Andreea who kept her apartment in the city as an investment property and moved to the farm as soon as possible.

▪

Shelly and her parents took a trip up to the farm for a week every summer, and for Christmas. This wavering in her fathers belief took place on one of their annual summer trips. The air had felt stale as it always had that summer when she was eight. This time however, it held a sort of stillness in it. As though time had stopped everywhere but the farm and they were living in some sort of bubble. It didn't feel like a safe bubble, where the outside world couldn't get at you, it felt more like someone was applying a constant slow pressure to your neck as the world slowly went dark. Shelly knew her father had felt it to because he shivered at the same time her and her mothers bodies stiffened. The moment they turned up the driveway. To the naked eye nothing was wrong. The stream which followed along the driveway and drained out into the pond was still a brilliant, shimmering blue. The ducks still sat in the pond and wandered around the garden. The fruit trees were in full bloom with flowers of many different colours. And the small stone farm house that sat at the end of the driveway was in the same condition it had always been in.

As they pulled up to the house Hank, her grandmothers dog came barrelling down the driveway to meet them. He was a funny looking dog, a mix of all sorts of things with a big fluffy coat and floppy ears. His tongue always seemed to be hanging out of his mouth with slobber dripping down its side. He was large, the size of a wolf Shelly imagined, but he was friendly.

They had parked the car and unpacked their bags. Shelly followed her parents as she always did, never running ahead to get to the house first. It wasn't that she wasn't excited to see her grandparents. She had always just had an eversion to the house. The floor boards creaked in a way that made it sound like there was always someone behind you or above you. The windows were beautiful, but only in the daylight. In the darkness that surrounded the farm at night due to its lack of street lights and neon restaurant signs it always felt as if a face would appear in front of you if you looked out just a second longer. You weren't allowed to wear shoes in the house in traditional Canadian fashion but the floors were cold and no socks could keep the cold from spreading to your whole body. Shelly had crinkled her toes up in her sneakers at the thought of it, as if trying to hold off the cold just a little bit longer. She soon forgot about that and the feeling of being watched when she saw her grandmother at the opened door. Her grandmother had always reminded her of the photos she had seen of Cecilia. A well built woman with tanned skin and long black hair that was often pulled back in a scarf. Her face was oval shaped, and her eyes were a deep brown. The scarf she had on that day in the door way was one that Shelly had picked out the year prior to give to her grandmother on her birthday. It was a deep green with golden magpies embroidered along its edges. She wore it so that it fell in a triangle along her hair, allowing the golden birds to shimmer as they caught the light. Shelly giggled when she saw it, and took off running to her grandmothers arms.

When Andreea's arms wrapped around Shelly they had felt frail compared to the strong muscular stocks she had so often attributed to her. Upon looking up at her Shelly also noticed something else, her face was thinner. She had frowned and then turned back to her parents who were just now reaching the front step.

"Aki," her grandmother moved to embrace her father. "I say this every year, but you need to start visiting more often." Their hug was brief, but filled with love, and she moved to wrap her arms tightly around her daughter.

"Maybe we should mom, you're looking thin. Is everything alright?" Shelly's mother pulled back from their embrace and now held tightly onto her own mother's hands.

"Oh Cosmina, you worry too much. It's just shadows you know, lurking in the dark. I keep them off." Andreea turned with this and motioned for them to come inside.

Cosmina looked up to stare at the centre of the door frame, and a slight frown found its way to her lips. Shelly followed her gaze, being at an age where she liked to mimic her, and felt a shiver pass through her. They stepped into the house and made their way to the kitchen where her grandfather sat.

"Grandpa Henry!" Shelly had squealed as she ran to jump into his lap.

Her fathers hand caught her shoulder, "careful Shelly-belly, you can't be jumping all over everyone all the time."

At that Henry had laughed and told her he might be old, but he wasn't as frail as her dad seemed to think. He had motioned for her to come give him a hug and she did so joyfully.

They had spent the remainder of the afternoon talking about the farm and finances and everything else adults seemed to feel the need to talk about after months of distance between them. Shelly had gotten bored of the conversation quickly and had went outside to play with Hank.

Shelly and Hank played together ever since she was big enough to walk. She would chase after him, and he would run in circles pretending she was fast and he was scared. When they had both run enough to warrant a well deserved nap they would curl up beside the pond and watch the ducks and the bees. But that had been when Shelly was young, eight was a time for exploring, not pond side naps. She had whistled to Hank in a half whistle half blowing of spit out of her mouth and he had bounded over to her side. She then raised her tree branch she had found into the air and dropped her arm to point it towards the forest.

-

"Attention!" She shouted, "its time to explore. It might be dangerous, but we have magic on our side" with this she waved the stick in the air and her and Hank marched off into the woods. After a few hundred yards there was another creek, slightly larger than the one that led into the duck pond. The water there was greener and lush plant life waved in its current. Shelly had made her way through the thick ferns of the Pacific Northwest forests and found her way to the edge of the creek. She knew there was a bridge somewhere near her grandparents place that Henry had taken her to the previous year to catch minnows off of. She stuck out her bottom lip as she looked up one side and down the other. Nothing. Hank had whimpered when she had turned to the right, so that must be the right way. She took off in that direction, staying close enough to the bank that she wouldn't lose the creek but not close enough that she might fall in. She had walked for what felt like miles, but in reality was probably only a couple hundred meters, and finally saw the bridge around a sharp bend in the creek. She giggled excitedly and called for Hank to hurry up as he had started to trail behind. He was getting older, but he wasn't old enough that he couldn't keep up with an eight year old kid. She reached the edge of the bridge and waited for Hank to catch up before crossing. She wouldn't go too much further in, just far enough that she might find a fairy ring or something else magical. She wandered around, poking the ground with her newly transformed wand, formerly tree branch, and felt something soft beneath one of the ferns. She poked again.

"Cut it out," the shrill voice of a young girl whispered from beneath the fern.

Shelly stepped back.

"What are y-"

"Shh!" The voice cut her off, and a hand reached out yanking Shelly's stick, and her to the ground. Hank had begun to let out a low growl but ceased when he heard another harsh shh!

"It took forever for me to find this spot. I always lose, and I'm not going to lose this time because you couldn't shut up."

Shelly was close enough now to see that the girl was close to her age, maybe a few years older but not by much. She laid on her belly to match the girl and shimmied over to push under the ferns with her. Hank circled them.

The little girl had pale skin and blueish pink lips. Her hair was fair and thin, but dirty giving it a sort of brown dust like colour. It hung wildly around her face which was full but pale where her cheeks should have been rosy from the heat. She wore a jumper and a light green t-shirt paired with white, recently muddied shoes. There looked to be deep gash on her neck, when Shelly had first glanced at her, but upon closer inspection there was nothing else there.

"I'm Hannah by the way," the girl whispered and shot Shelly a big grin that seemed empty of any actual friendliness.

"I'm not supposed to talk to strangers," Shelly had begun to inch away, almost sure the gash had been there, rotating between Hannah's face and her neck, "are - are you okay?"

"Why wouldn't I be?"

"Well, you're on the ground in the forest and there's no one else out here?" Shelly had gotten out from under the ferns now and sat up, looking around the forest cautiously as Hank still circled.

"Yes there is, my brothers are out here."

"Well, I don't see anyone."

Now it was Hannah's turn to sit up. She looked around the forest and huffed, "they left me." Her look of disappointment was soon replaced by that wide grin, "that means I won!"

She turned again to look out at the forest as Shelly turned to look back at her, there it was again, the gash. She only saw it briefly but it was there.

"I should uh.. probably get going."

"What? No, stay! I won that means I get to be queen of the castle. Come see our tree fort with me it's not far." The tone in Hannah's voice sounded strange, and Shelly had never seen a fort on any of her and her grandfathers walks.

"No I'm - "

"I want you to stay," Hannah had grabbed Shelly's arm. Her grip was tighter than any ten year old girl should be capable of. But her strength wasn't what concerned Shelly. What made her skin feel tight on her bones was how cold Hannah's hand was, and the look of hunger in her eyes as she looked at Shelly. Shelly pulled back and screamed just as Hank rushed at Hannah, his teeth barred. She dropped Shelly's arm and moved to cover her own face from Hank's barreling body. He crashed into her and didn't stop as Shelly staggered to her feet and the two took off running back across the bridge.

"Hey! Wait! I didn't mean to scare you please come back!" Hannah's voice called out, sounding sweet and delicate as it followed them through the trees. "Please, I'm sorry." She had begun running after them now, Shelly could hear her as she stumbled through the ferns and fallen trees.

▪

They had reached the bridge and crossed it as quickly as they could manage, Hank following behind her. She could still hear the other girl behind them but she didn't stop even as the breath began to catch in her throat. Her and Hank were nearly home now and the footsteps that had been behind them didn't seem to be following since they had crossed the bridge. Still, the blood was pounding in her veins and the air around Hank felt uneasy and dark so she kept running. Hank had began to fall behind but Shelly couldn't stop, knew she couldn't, even if it meant leaving Hank. Tears had started to run down her cheeks and she could hear Hank slowing down. By the time she reached the door she could no longer hear him behind her and the tears had started to flow in a steady stream. She burst through the back door into the living room and collapsed, breathing hard. Cosmina rushed to her and asked her what happened and where Hank was.

"There was a - a girl... grabbed me... lost Hank." Shelly was sobbing now, and hardly audible between breaths.

"What was her name?"

"Hannah." She curled up into her mothers chest and cried for Hank.

Andreea had moved to stand beside her daughter and Shelly, a worried look passing over her face, "that was one of them. The shadows."

"Oh. Andreea no." It was Aki who spoke now as he moved towards Andreea, motioning for her to sit back down.

"A sh-shadow?" Shelly's tears had stopped but the quiver in her voice was still there as she looked up towards her grandma, "what's the shadows?"

"That's what she was dear, they are like demons. They make you sick, like they're doing to me. They watch you and they latch on and try and take the life from you. Poor Hank." The words caught in her throat as she thought about her beloved dog.

"Andreea, I think you should go lay down. You aren't feeling well. Look, there's Hank right there," Aki motioned out the window to where Hank now stood panting at the edge of the forest. He trotted over to the door and Aki let him inside.

Andreea fell to her knees and wrapped her arms around him as tears began to well in her eyes, "oh Hank! The shadows, they didn't take you after all."

Hank licked her face then pulled away and walked over to Shelly, nuzzling her arm.

"Come now dear," Henry had stood up from his place in his wooden rocking chair beside the fire place, "Aki's right you

should lay down." He gently reached for her elbow and guided Andreea down the hall.

"Dad, what's the shadows?

"Shelly, grandma's sick. That's what mommy and grandpa and grandma and I have been discussing. She has a disease, its called Alzheimer's and it makes grandma confused. She doesn't always know what she's talking about. Does that make sense?"

Shelly felt her mothers arms tighten around her when her father mentioned the disease.

"Yah, that makes sense. My teacher told us about Alzheimer's, old people get it. But grandma said that the shadows are what make her sick?"

"I know dear, but she's just confused and maybe trying to make sense of it all. The shadows aren't real, and the little girl you met in the woods is probably just one of the neighbours kids. Now I think its time we got ready for bed okay? The suns starting to go down and mommy and daddy are tired."

"I think sleep sounds like a fantastic idea," Cosmina kissed Shelly on top of her head and stood up, pulling Shelly up with her.

The next few days were uneventful. Shelly and Hank decided that perhaps their usual activities of napping by the duck pond and playing chase were their best options for fun. The grown ups continued to have long chats, sometimes in the living room, sometimes on the patio while Henry cooked hot dogs on the barbecue. It was the fourth day that Shelly noticed the waver in her fathers belief of purely science and logic.

Shelly had spent the day as usual, napping with Henry by the pond and chasing him around with the ducks. She had come in late when the sun has begun to set and sat down to eat the dinner that had been left out for her. Andreea had come into the kitchen and stood beside the window, the big one that Shelly always made sure not to look at. Outside had begun to dim and a pale orange light had begun to shine through it, lighting the kitchen in a soft haze.

"How's that pasta tasting Shelly-belly?"

"It's good dad, thank you."

Her father had come into the kitchen and now stood adjacent to Shelly and her grandmother, forming a small triangle between them.

Her grandmother hadn't said a word since she had come into the kitchen, and since it was not yet dark out Shelly thought it was probably safe to look up to where her she was standing. Thats when she saw it. In the window pane, just over Andreea's right shoulder was a large dark shadow. It looked to be in the shape of a man but its edges had a jagged sort of feeling to them. It had one arm, if a person could call it that, clasped to Andreea's shoulder. And even though it had no face, Shelly couldn't help but feel that it was starring at her, and grinning in the same way that the girl from the woods had.

She dropped her fork and there was a loud clang, "Grandma... is that a shadow?"

She saw her father turn, and heard the water pitcher he had been filling in the sink beginning to overflow. And she knew he could see it to, because his eyes were fixed in exactly the place the looming blackness stood beside her grandmother.

Chapter 4

what it's like to mourn

The day had finally come. Shelly taped up the last of her boxes and piled them into a corner for the movers to haul downstairs and into their large white moving contraption that looked like someone had welded a shipping container onto a mini semi truck and called it a day. She placed her hands on her hips and did one last look around her old room. A heavy sigh escaped her as her eyes came to rest on the window that overlooked the city street. She made her way over and looked out at the neon signs that lit up China town only a few blocks away. She scanned the street for the man in the blue jacket, something she had made a habit of since that night three years ago. She couldn't shake the feeling that he knew something she didn't, could see something she didn't. She often felt a second pair of eyes watching over her shoulder when she searched for him and thought they were the reason he stayed away. The reason for the look of sorrow as his eyes met hers. Maybe he was like her mom and could see things others couldn't, or maybe he was one of the things others couldn't see. She doubted that though. She couldn't see those things either, aside from that day at the farm.

Something brushed against her leg, dragging itself in a snake like pattern. Shelly screamed and jumped back from the window.

HSSSS

"Oh my gosh. I'm sorry jibbles. You scared the shit out of me."

Shelly bent down and picked up her cat. He was a large fluffy thing who seemed to have constant matts under his arms no matter how often she trimmed, brushed, and cut them out. He left tufts of white and brown fur all around the house that were often mistaken for spiders and make her father scream when they rolled across the floor to him.

She stroked his fur and kissed his head as she stepped back to the window. They looked out together, admiring the city they would no longer be calling home.

"Funny isn't it Jibbles? We've lived her our whole lives and I still feel like theres so much about this place I don't know. So many things I haven't seen or experinced. You probably feel that way all the time hey? Couped up in this house, only seeing the world through a couple of windows."

Jibbles just sat there, his eyes transfixed on a pigeon that sat on the power line outside of Shelly's room.

"Don't worry about Jibbles."

Her father stood in the doorway, leaning casually against the frame, one arm behind his back. Hiding something.

"Maybe he'll learn to be a fierce hunter and explorer and you guys can go see what's hiding in the woods or hang out at the beach together."

With that the cat jumped from Shelly's arms and plopped himself onto the ground. He arched his back, stretched his tail up rudely in Shelly's direction and curled up to nap at her feet.

Aki chuckled and shook his head at the complete lack of regard the cat ever seemed to give anyone, "Ya, I didn't think so. Which is why.." He stepped into the room, his arm still behind him, "I got a backup plan."

He took another step, then another leading a dog into the room on a bright yellow leash.

Shelly's mouth dropped open, Jibbles raised his head and blinked lazily at the dog before going back to his nap, "Edward!"

Shelly stepped over Jibbles and ran to the dog, wrapping her arms around his huge fluffy neck. He nuzzled into her as he had in the dream and licked her face. She kissed him between the eyes as she stood up and flung her arm around her father's shoulders, squeezing him tightly.

"Thank you, dad."

-

They stood at the front door of the apartment. Aki and Cosmina directed the movers on where to go and what to move first. "Start with the boxes in the bedroom, then the kitchen, then the office and furniture last."

Aki had assured Cosmina they were professionals and knew how to move and pack some boxes and furniture but she wasn't willing to risk any mess ups.

Shelly tied her shoes, zipped up her jacket, and made sure Edward's collar was snug enough he wouldn't get out of it but also loose enough he wouldn't be uncomfortable. She couldn't even wear a turtle neck so she was sure a collar being on all the time probably wasn't all that fun either.

"We're gonna go out for a walk and meet up with Sal and Kyra for a bit," she half called out over her shoulder as she opened the door to leave. Edward was already ahead of her, ready to bound down the nine flights of stairs ahead of them.

"Woah. Hey wait a minute," Cosmina grabbed the door and stopped Shelly, "do you remember everything your dad told you? And what time you HAVE to be back by?"

"Yes," Shelly sighed and rolled her eyes without any real attitude so Cosmina let it slide. "Edward's trained but we don't know exactly how well so don't let him go off leash. Don't let him pull me around, give him treats to get him to walk beside me. Don't let strangers pet him cause you never know how he'll react. And we have to leave by two thirty so be back by no later than two fifteen."

"And?"

"And??"

"And I love you."

"I love you too mom, can I go now?"

"Have fun, tell them I said hi."

Shelly waved over her shoulder as Edward started down the stairs and Cosmina closed the door behind her, leaving

Shelly with the muffled sound of her directing the movers to be careful with their artwork.

"I guess stairs it is, you seem adamantly against the elevator huh?"

Edward barked and continued his descent.

▪

The street was busy for a Tuesday, an odd day to move, but it was the cheapest day to get the movers so Tuesday it was. Businessmen in navy blue suits and brown polished dress suits walked quickly through the street, phones pressed to their ears. She often thought of how they seemed to be dickheads about people working hard and putting in the hours yet seemed to have some of the worst time management skills she'd ever seen. How could a person always look so rushed and frantic if they were supposed to be the best and the smartest? Ha, yeah, like she'd ever believe that about a guy who looked like every other white frat bro on the planet. Business men, no thank you. Then there were the film students. Gastown had square foot upon square foot of studios and film schools beneath the city streets and piled on top of one another in heritage buildings that were only heritage on the outside. They liked to sit outside and smoke, dressed better and cooler than most people in Vancouver, or at least they liked to think so. They always seemed to separate themselves into groups she had noticed. There were the queer kids, the ones who were actually cool and well dressed, usually noticeable by their love of tattoos and bright-coloured clothes, or lack thereof. The students of colour often overlapped with the queer kids, the other groups didn't really let them in unless they fit their mould. Then there were the film bros who were essentially guys who thought they were better than the businessmen cause they were creative but they hadn't had an original idea, ever. They were guys who would most likely make it cause they were young and white and the societal standard of handsome even though they wore fake glasses and nail polish and thought that somehow made them unique. Then there was the white feminists, people whose entire identity in film revolved around "making a difference" but they only worked with white writers, the occasional diversity black kid, and an all white, all Canadian crew.

Sal was a part of the queer kids group, they loved film and music and art. They were an incredible director and an even more incredible musician. Shelly went to all of their shows and photographed them when they weren't looking so they wouldn't shy away, an odd trait for someone who was going to be famous one day. Shelly thought Sal was the most beautiful person she had ever seen, and for someone who hated being photographed, the most bold. Sal had beautiful long dark hair that was full and voluminous like a Disney princess or someone out of a Pantene commercial. They exclusively wore see-through tops with X's taped in bright neon across their nipples. Since they had breasts the school still wouldn't allow their nipples to show, and they decided to compromise. A symbol of resistance against the status quo, against the institutions that confine us to one body and one identity of personhood, Sal would say, and then add with a nudge of Shelly's arm and a wink, "plus, I know you like to look."

They had a prominent nose that jutted outwards as if to say look at me now fuckers and try and tell me I'm not beautiful, she had the same brown eyes as Shelly did and they would often get high and stare into the others, trying to see if they could somehow seem themselves through the others. Their skin was dark and they kept the hair long on their arms and legs. They strutted in high heels and army pants, wore combat boots with mini skirts, and always had a signature neon highlighter that matched the X's under their shirt.

Sal sat outside now, waiting for Shelly and chatting with their film friends. Today they wore a white mesh shirt with hot pink X's and hot pink liner to match, black flared jeans that began the flare at the hips, and white platform heart stomper boots. Shelly took out her phone and snapped a picture. Sal's arms moved in the typical director's fashion, always ready to tell someone what to do to elevate the scene, even a scene as simple as living one's daily life.

"I saw that," Sal grinned a large full face sort of grin that lit up the world. Shelly swooned every time she saw it.

Sal walked to her and wrapped her up in their arms. Shelly couldn't help but notice how Sal pushed their hips into her and she felt the blood rushing to meet them.

She pulled back and patted Edward on the head, "this is Edward."

"Oh. My. God! I'm obsessed. Edward you beautiful handsome man!" Sal sunk down to a squat and kissed Edward on the nose, "whose the best boy?" They squeezed his cheeks and he barked a happy bark, "yes exactly. You know you are, yes you are!"

Sal stood back up to look at Shelly, "he's adorable. Just like you, you're perfect for each other."

Shelly blushed at Sal's compliment, "should we go get Kyra?"

"Hell yeah," Sal turned back to her smoke team, "cover for me?"

A thumbs up was the only response they received, "they're so good to me."

-

Kyra worked at a small bookstore at the other end of the downtown area of the city, near sunset beach and was about a 20-minute bus ride away. Sal, however, refused to take the bus and had called an Uber instead. Too many gawking men on the bus they said, and they weren't wrong.

"Thanks," they said in unison as they exited the vehicle, letting Edward hop out onto the sidewalk first.

Kyra stood waiting outside of the bookshop, fashion magazine in hand, leaning against the concrete wall she convinced the shop to paint entirely black. She was goth on the inside she would say, she just preferred the aesthetic of a barbie doll on her body. She had lip filler and micro-bladed eyebrows with a set of full lashes to match. She always had some sort of pink involved in her outfit and today it was the whole thing. Pink leather skirt, pink fluffy top not unlike the Austin Power Fembots, and bright pink new balance sneakers. The shoes were the only part of the barbie aesthetic she couldn't do. Heels were the bane of her existence, but what she lacked in stilleto, she made up for in legs. She was the tallest of the three by a mile, clocking in at nearly 6 feet tall. Her parent's always thought she should've been a basketball girl but she much preferred hockey and wasn't wrong about her height being an advantage. She was a varsity athlete, a book nerd, a goth, and a barbie all rolled into one, and guys hated that about her. They didn't like that she was so confident and sure of herself, that she knew exactly who she was and refused to conform to a single box like they wanted her to. She always said that's why she stuck with them, her friends since elementary school because they were better than any guy would ever be for her. Plus, she just really didn't understand the whole appeal of sex. Shelly and Sal would always give each other a sideways glance when she said this, and she always noticed but didn't feel like she was ready to label herself with anything so she always pretended not to.

"You must be Edward! Shelly, I was just dying at that snap you sent, he's fricking gorgeous." She rubbed his head and gave him a boop on the nose.

"Oh hey, nice nip covers, we're matching."

"Yeah but I wear it better, hey Shelly?" Another arm nudge.

"I don't know, Kyra's looking pretty hot."

They all laughed for a second before it faded into a melancholy sort of aching sound and then drowned into nothing. The realization that this was the last time they would be able to spend time together so easily settled over them and it was Sal who finally broke the silence.

"Well, are we doing this or what? Edward deserves to experience the spectacular Stanley Park before he's hauled off to live on an island paradise."

"You sure you can manage that in those boots?" Kyra wiggled her new balance's at Sal's feet.

"Okay yeah, I forgot to dress for the occasion, shoot me."

Shelly and Kyra gave Sal a skeptical look.

"I'll be fine, lets's hit it."

▪

The group walked along the sea wall for a while in silence, taking in the sun on their faces and the sounds of the ocean as it lapped up against the stone wall. Edward pranced happily ahead of them, tugging only slightly on his leash. When they came to one of the forest entrances Shelly told Edward to sit and bent down to look him in the eyes. He smiled back at her, tail wagging and tongue hanging out the side of his mouth.

"If I let you off leash can you be good?"

Edward stared at her and cocked his head to one side.

"Seems like a yes to me," Kyra said and she and Sal both shrugged as Shelly looked at them for a decision.

"Okay, I'm trusting you."

She reached down and unclipped Edward's leash. He continued to sit and look at her and she smiled to herself with a look of unearned satisfaction.

"Okay," she clapped, "let's go."

Edward walked by her side as they went through the forest, only leaving every so often to follow a scent or a stray squirrel and never leaving the path or Shelly's sight.

"So what do you think it's gonna be like?" Sal sounded serious, not in a concerned sort of way, but in a way that showed she was going to miss Shelly.

"I don't know really. I've only seen a couple of photos of the outside of the house. My mom forgot to take pictures when

she went to see it but she said it's really nice. It was only built a couple of years ago, and I guess the guy who built it thought it was too creepy or something so he left."

"Creepy?"

"Did your mom say she saw anything or felt anything ... off ... about it?"

"No actually, she said she just thinks it's cause he build a house in the middle of a forest with an entire wall for a window and didn't put in any curtains.

"Oh man, that is creepy."

"Exactly. But she said aside from that it's pretty cool. There's even a pool and a room in the basement they're going to let me turn into a dark room. Plus I get my own full-size bathroom which'll be nice."

The other two nodded and then Sal stopped.

"Hey, I've gotta pee. Shelly you wanna come with?"

Shelly looked at Edward and then into the forest.

"Don't worry, I've got him. Edward sit," Kyra pointed to the ground, "see, he listens perfectly well to me."

"Yah, sure, okay."

▪

Sal and Shelly made their way into the forest, careful not to disturb nature too much, they both came from families and cultures that valued and cared for the environment and were always careful to abide by its rules. When they found a big tree Sal stopped and turned to Shelly. They grabbed her waist and pulled her in quickly, pressing their lips to hers. Shelly grabbed at Sal's waist and pulled their hips into hers, her back pushing up against the tree. Sal's tongue flicked inside her mouth and their hand left Shelly's waist, finding its way undershirt and grabbing her boob. They squeezed and Shelly moaned as Sal pushed her thigh between Shelly's legs. Shelly fumbled for the button of Sal's jeans, popped it open, unzipped the zipper and shoved her hand into Sal's underwear. Sal pushed into her further and Shelly slid her fingers into Sal. Sal followed suit and did the same.

They breathed heavily and Sal said in between kisses, "I've always wanted to do this, I thought... I'd have... more time."

"You can always... come... visit."

-

Kyra sat on her phone and crouched beside Edward who sat perfectly still aside from his wagging tail.

"You think they're making out in their Eddy? I hope so, it's taken them long enough. I mean how many times can they flirt and practically undress each other with their eyes at the fricking dinner table before they hop into bed togeth-"

She stopped as the forest darkened and Edward stood up, his hackles raised and a low growl began to escape his throat. Kyra looked up, no clouds. Hmm, weird. She thought, she was sure the forest was noticeably darker. She stood up and looked around. The birds had stopped singing and not even the sound of the city reached her anymore. It was as though a glass dome had fallen over her and stifled the world. "Shelly?" She called out, "Sal?"

The hairs on the back of her neck and her arms stood up, she shivered and shook it off, attributing it to the dimming sun and the chill that must have brought.

The growl grew louder, more defensive and then Edward was gone. He took off towards the forest where Shelly and Sal had disappeared to.

"Shit!" Kyra followed, thankful for the runners she was wearing, "Edward! Hey Edward stop!"

-

The forest darkened and nature halted. Sal and Shelly froze, carefully untangling themselves from the other. Sal buttoned their pants and Shelly hers, readjusting her shirt as well.

"There weren't any clouds today. Were there?"

"No, there weren't."

"So why's it so dark?"

Shadows. Shelly thought to herself. She hadn't thought about them in a long while. Not since the trip to the farm when she was eight. Her grandma had gained her weight back and hadn't mentioned them since. She was perfectly healthy as far as Shelly knew and her parents had assured her it was a trick of the light and her grandmother's sickness had gotten to her head. And she had believed them, sort of, but she remembered the figure so clearly, the way it latched onto her grandmother's shoulders, and towered above her. The way it had somehow smiled at her with no face, a hungry smile, a wanting and knowing smile. It knew something she didn't, like the man in the blue jacket.

"Edward!" Kyra's voice was the only sound to break the silence, it was muffled and quiet, further away than it should have been, but still, it was her and she was calling for Edward.

Shelly and Sal stepped out from behind the tree and were nearly plowed through by Edward who was growling and barking wildly as he tore passed them like they weren't even there.

Shelly and Sal looked at each other before they took off after him. The forest grew darker the further in they went and the air was stale the way it had been when she was eight. Sal fell behind in their platform heels but Shelly couldn't stop, she was being propelled forward, towards her dog and towards something else that she was not aware of.

"Edward!" She cupped her hands around her mouth as she ran, trying to project her voice, to command him, she needed him to stop before he got to it, whatever it was. "Edward stop! Come here! Sit Edward, please! Stop!"

And he did.

He stopped in a pile of ferns in a small opening of the forest. The air was so still, so dense that Shelly thought she might not be able to breathe if she stayed here much longer.

She stepped cautiously as Edward began to whimper, he circled and sniffed around the ferns with his hackles still raised as she made her way to him.

"Edward", her voice shook as she reached out to stroke his back and calm him, "hey, it's okay."

She didn't believe that and she knew that he knew she was bluffing. She pulled the leash from around her neck, slowly so as to not startle him. He continued to sniff the ground, unaware of her. She pressed the clip and moved to catch the loop on his collar.

And then she was falling and kicking. Kicking at the cold fleshy hand that was locked onto her ankle, kicking at the face that smirked at her from the grass. Another hand reached up and covered her mouth, she bit at it but its grip never wavered. Then another hand on her shoulder, and another, and another. She was sinking, being pulled down into the earth. Tree roots tangled themselves around her wrists as her feet sank completely into the once soft mulch covered ground that now seemed to be as hard as stone.

"Hi!" The face of the boy that drug her was suddenly above her. He pressed his weight into her and she screamed as he bent down to hover above her tears.

She gagged when he opened his mouth and the stench of decay and rot blew past his teeth. His skin was purple and yellowed with decay, falling from his bones above his eyes, his shoulder, and his stomach. His insides pushed out of him and were wet against her skin, his legs and fingers were bloated to match his throat which was blue and rotten.

"You haven't seen my sister by any chance. Have ya shelly?"

She shook her head as best she could under the hand that still trapped her.

He threw his head back and laughed. He bent down and whispered something in her ear in a language she didn't understand, or maybe it was that his words were so gargled and choked that she couldn't make the words out.

Then he was gone, and so were the roots and the hands and the dirt that weighed her down. She scrambled backwards and Edward made his way to stand over her. She buried her face into his side and clung to him as she cried.

Sal and Kyra burst into the clearing as the sun began to poke through the darkened air. Sal bent down and put their hands on their knees and breathed heavily. Kyra patted their back and pulled down her skirt before walking towards Shelly.

"Hey.. Shelly, you alright?"

Shelly looked up and pulled her face away from Edward, his long hair clinging to her tears. She wiped at them and gave her shoulders a shake.

"Yah, I'm all right. Just was happy to catch him, I thought he was gone."

Sal caught their breath and made their way to their friends. They looked skeptically at Shelly's messed-up hair and dirt covered body.

"So.. why ya covered in dirt?"

"Oh umm," Shelly stood up and brushed the dirt off of her legs, Kyra took it upon herself to dust down her back, "I just fell, tripped over a rock or something. It was quite a tumble."

Sal nodded, unsure of why Shelly would lie, "I see. Must have been to have that much dirt on you."

Kyra looked between them as Shelly met Sal's gaze. She wanted to tell Sal everything but she couldn't and she knew if she didn't hold firm that Sal would never let it go.

"All right, now that we've had some adventure why don't we find some ice cream or something?" Kyra fiddled with her thumbs as she said it, as perfect as she was, she picked her thumbs to the point of tears and sores.

Shelly pulled out her phone. 1:50. How had that happened so quickly?

"Fuck, I've gotta go, guys. I'm so sorry."

"What already?" Sal had softened and panic flashed across their eyes with the thought of that being their last interaction with Shelly.

Shelly held up her phone and showed them the time which caused confusion and slight unease to pass between them all.

They walked quickly out of the forest or as quickly as they could with Sal now barefoot and carrying the impractical platforms. They called an Uber and piled in. Unwilling and unable to speak they sat in silence.

▪

The car pulled up to Shelly's house at 2:25 and her parents were outside waiting. Her dad looked pissed, her mom less so. But her mom looked strange, her face red and splotchy and her dad's eyes seemed puffy around the edges. Had they been crying? She chalked it up to moving and leaving their home behind, if something had happened they would have told her, and would have called.

Just as before Edward hopped out first, followed by Shelly, then Kyra, then Sal. There was no thank you this time as the silence followed them out onto the street.

"Well," her dad crossed his arms, "say goodbye, we need to get going." Then he softened his stance slightly and looked at her friends, "I'm sorry it's such a rushed goodbye girls, you're welcome to visit anytime."

Cosmina stepped forward and hugged Kyra and Sal, "we're going to miss you guys."

"We'll miss you too," they hugged her back and then turned to Shelly who stood slumped with Edward tucked neatly against her leg.

Kyra hugged her first, squeezing her tightly as tears filled both of their eyes, "don't forget about us okay? And don't forget to write."

"What is this the 1950s?"

"It's an expression okay. Even though it would be kind of cool to be pen pals."

They laughed and squeezed each other again before Kyra stepped away to make room for Sal who reached for Shelly's cheek and wiped off her tears, "none of that. But Kyra's right. Don't forget about us. I'll be pissed if I show up to visit and you don't know who I am. What a waste of a ferry ticket."

Shelly choked on her laugh this time as she told Sal to shut up. They hugged and Sal whispered in her ear, "call me tonight okay? We need to talk about that."

Shelly nodded against Sal's cheek and pulled away. She didn't turn back as she made her way to the car and loaded Edward into the back seat beside Jibble's carrier and crawled in behind him. She looked dead ahead as her parents got in the car and her dad started the engine. She let out a shakey breath as the tears began to streak down her cheeks in gutting waves. She looked back at her friends once more, hoping to see them again soon, or ever.

Chapter 5

a new home

The ferry ride hadn't been terrible, nothing special, nothing of note. Still, Shelly couldn't but watch the sky, waiting for it to darken, and when the sun shifted positions in the sky and cast shadows where they hadn't been before it made her squirm. The sea was calm, and the sky still cloudless. Edward and Jibbles were perfectly content to let the boat rock them to sleep. Her parents had made their way to the passenger deck for a late lunch but she had opted to stay in the car. Edward would know if something was wrong, granted her mother most likely would as well, but she found comfort in the fact that Edward displayed his distrust so clearly.

▪

After nearly three hours the ferry had docked and they were on their way to their new home. The house her parents had bought was at the north end of the island in a place called Fernwood. It was close to a lake, St. Mary Lake if a person wanted to be specific. That suited her she had thought when she searched up the location. She had always been more of a lake person, not that she didn't like the ocean, but a lake held comfort in its waters. She often longed for the moments of serenity when she could wade into the lakes in the north by her grandparent's farm; and lay on her back and float. The world and everything in it seemed to be absorbed into the water and all sense became trivial. She smiled at the thought of taking Sal and Kyra there when they came to visit if they ever did. What are you saying, of course, they're coming. She couldn't let the intrusive thoughts in. The thoughts of loneliness, of abandonment. She wasn't sure where they even came from. Her parents had always been amazing, they had loved her and supported her in everything. When she was depressed in her grade ten year they had been understanding and patient. They took her to therapy and went to group sessions to better understand how to help her. They held her through her journey with medication and the incredible lows when she came off of them. She couldn't have asked for a better family. And her friends were wonderful too. They had only ever gotten into one fight and none of them could even remember what it was about anymore. There was more depth between them than if all the chasms and crevices from mountain to ocean had been stacked on top of one another. And yet, she couldn't help but feel an overwhelming sense of loneliness.

▪

"We're here!" Her parent's voices always seemed to ring out in perfect harmony together. She wondered if she would ever find that. She liked Sal, maybe even loved Sal non-platonically, but they didn't seem in unison. Perhaps unison was something you grew into when your souls truly connected. She hadn't been there at the start of her parent's relationship so for all she knew they were awkward and ill-prepared for their first encounter outside of the courtship dance as well.

She sat up in her seat, peering out the window for a better look, "are you sure?"

There was nothing but forest and a neatly packed dirt road stretched out in front of them. The trees towered overhead and created a shaded canopy where spotlights of sun shone through and the largest ferns she had ever seen sprung out of the ground. She pulled away from them, leaning into Edward.

Her mother turned around to look at her through her and her husband's seats. She grabbed Shelly's knee and squeezed, "everything okay hun?"

"Yah, everything's fine. Just.. not used to everything yet."

Cosmina nodded her head and pulled her lips into a tight smile. She searched her daughter's face but couldn't find what she had been looking for. In silence, she turned back around and stared out the window of her own door.

Then the trees began to thin and the forest gave way to a beautiful opening of tall grass and wildflowers of at least half an acre. A freshly made log fence lined the property and at the edge of it sat the ocean. Shelly's mood brightened as she saw how the sun danced off the water and the flowering meadow swayed in the slight ocean breeze. In the center of the property sat the house. It was a long rectangle once made of shipping containers. Large windows lined the walls, and a bright blue door sat in the center of it. The driveway within the property had been sheeted with large chunks of gravel that crunched under the tires, waking the sleeping animals next to Shelly. Edward stretched into her and pushed her against the door, she pushed him back and he sat down neatly next to her, admiring his new home.

They parked and unloaded the few things they had packed into the car. The movers wouldn't be there for another hour. Something about them having to catch a later ferry because of weight, she hadn't really been paying attention. She let Edward off his leash and set Jibbles's carrier down and opened the door. Jibbles peeked his head out, looked at her like she was bat shit crazy if she thought he was going out there, then popped back into the safety of the ridiculous backpack she had bought to take him on adventures with her. She adjusted her potted aloe vera and the camera bag she had slung over her shoulder and looked at her parents who were making their way from the car. Aki carried some small paintings under his arm and a tackle kit that held his most expensive paints, Cosmina, a large metal case that contained her tattoo machines. Her father jingled the keys at her with his free hand and shuffled passed her to the door. He turned around and bowed, making a show of unlocking the door to their new home, then placed the key in the lock, turned it, and swung the door open.

Edward pushed them both out of the way and rushed into the foyer, her father followed, accompanied by her mother, while she tried to coax Jibbles out of his carrier.

"Jibbles, come here," she spoke in a soft and high-pitched tone while she rubbed her fingers at him, "come on buddy."

He wouldn't even look at her and she gave up easily, "fine." She picked up the bag and took him inside, where he immediately jumped out of the open hatch and disappeared upstairs. The house was two stories, more like one but the basement technically counted since it was only half underground. The house had been built on a hill and the backside of the house had had the hillside cut out around it allowing for the basement to feel homier and have natural light. This was where the bedrooms were. On the backside, along the wall with no windows a long hallway stretched the length of the house and at its end was the only room with no windows, and no daylight, the room Shelly could turn into a dark room. Beside that was her bathroom attached directly to her room. Next to her room was her parent's bathroom which was attached to their room. The upper floor of the house contained a garage which they would most likely use for storage. On the backside of the garage was a large pantry and a kitchen that had been done in all white, a style her mother detested and was already figuring out how to gut and redo. Next to the kitchen was a small dining area with a large black brick wall separating it from the living room. The living room overlooked the water and the steep incline that led down to the small sandy beach below it that was only reachable by the thousands of steps the previous owner had custom-built. Behind the living room, on the other side of the stairs that had been oddly placed in the center of what would be described as a hallway had it not been so open concept, was a large space her father planned on turning into his studio. On the patio that stretched out from the living room was a pool in the shape of an oval with a hot tub placed inside of it by the far right corner. It looked almost like a paint pallet.

Shelly made her way around the house, her pets following along behind her. Edward really didn't mind Jibbles, and

Jibbles couldn't have cared less about the dog so they had no problem being near Shelly when the other was there. As she wandered her parents made their way through the French collapsing doors onto the patio. They stood with their arms wrapped around each other with her mother's head resting on her father's shoulder and his head resting on her temple. They stayed like that until Shelly came back upstairs.

"The moving truck's not gonna be here for a little while, do you want to come to check out the town? See my new studio? Maybe help me figure out how to upgrade the sign. I'm so tired of all those boring tattoo guys and their stupid monster energy fonts. We get it, you're hardcore, right?"

"Yeah, that sounds fun. Can I bring Edward?"

Her father patted Edward on the head as he walked back into the house behind his wife and closed the door, "its probably better if Eddy stays here Shelly Belly, we'll probably get some dinner and he's not gonna want to sit in the car."

She didn't like it, but she knew her father was right so she gave Edward a pat and followed her parents out the front door. Her dad locked it behind them and started towards the car. Cosmina grabbed Shelly's arm and stopped her for a moment.

"Hey," she tucked Shelly's hair behind her ear, "I've been all over this island and there's nothing here okay? No heebie jeebies." Then she levelled her voice, something she only did when she needed Shelly to listen, "and no children in the woods, nothing like that. Okay?"

Shelly just stared at her. Had she known about what happened in the woods somehow?

"Shelly, I need you to answer me and tell me you understand what I'm saying. We've left those things behind us. Can you do that, can you leave them behind us." She was asking, but she wasn't, it was more like telling Shelly she need to forget and move on.

"Okay, yeah yeah," Shelly shook her head as though trying to throw the memories out of it, "yeah I can do that."

"Okay great." And with that, she stood up and walked to the car.

Shelly waited a moment, watching her. Her mother had never been someone to avoid problems and certainly not someone to essentially say forget what you saw and don't ever speak about it again. She brushed it off, chalked it up to wanting a fresh start and followed her parents to the car.

▪

The drive to town was longer than Shelly had expected. It followed a winding road that cut through the dense forest. Every once in a while the glint of the ocean would shine through the trees, or there would be an opening with another house, but mostly it was just forest.

"There's a girl that's your age who lives next door, Shelly." Her mother had turned around again to chat, she wasn't one to speak without looking directly at a person, said she couldn't hear her own thoughts if she wasn't and then she wouldn't know what to say.

"Is there such a thing as next door?"

Her fathered laughed and Cosmina gave him a playful punch in the arm. He fake winced and rubbed the spot her arm had hit.

"Yes, there's such a thing as next door. It's just on the other side of the trees, to the left. I met her and her dad's when I came to see the house. They're really nice. She's going to school to be a chemical engineer after she graduates isn't that something? I told her you were into photography and she said there's some really cool places that she could show you that might be cool to take some pictures at. Oh, and both her dad's are architects! That's how they met. They were both hired to work on this house in Iceland, they build and design custom homes so that's pretty cool. But anyways, they we're working on this house and met each other and instantly clicked. They said that right away they felt like they were perfectly in sync and *that to this day it's the best thing either of them has ever designed. We'll have to invite them over sometime. Hey Aki?"*

"Yes, definitely they sound like very interesting people. And it would be nice for you to meet someone your age here, hey Shelly?"

"Yeah, that would be cool."

All Shelly could think of was Sal, how their lips had felt against hers, how the calluses on their hand had scrapped against her nipple and how they repeated the movement when they could tell she liked it. She thought about how she had fumbled so pathetically with Sal's button and wondered if they felt pleasure from the way she had fingered them the way she had when Sal so effortlessly slid their hand down the front of her jeans. Then her heart started to gain speed as she thought back to how effortless that was, had Sal been doing that with other people too? Did all Sal want was to fuck her and is that why they said they'd been wanting to do that for so long? Would they be thinking of her tonight when they were alone as well? What did this mean for their friendship and had they wanted to call and talk to tell her it didn't mean anything? She had been staring out the window, watching the trees go by and then she saw him. Standing just off the side of the road. The boy from the forest, his skin was rotting from his face and his legs and hands bloated, he was fully naked which she hadn't noticed before and he smiled at her, the same way the shadow had that day at the farm. She tore her eyes from him and met her mother's gaze in the side mirror. She held Shelly there, her jaw clenched. Then Shelly turned her head and closed her eyes.

▪

"Hey, earth to Shelly," her dad waved his hand in front of her face, "hello."

"What?" Her eyes opened and she pushed her dad's hand away.

"We're here. Welcome to town."

The town was small but larger than she had pictured it so that counted for something. There was one main street and quite a few side streets that were the homes of bed and breakfasts, small artisan shops, and old-timey homes with well-kept lawns. The main street was home to the larger artisan shops, an art gallery and a few higher end studios, a grocery store, a dentist and doctor's office, a post office, a bakery, some tourist shops, and restaurants with hours that didn't make much sense. The Italian restaurant was only open until 2:00 pm, the Greek restaurant was open from 1:00 - 5:00 pm on weekdays and 1:00 pm - 7:00 pm on weekends, the Indian restaurant was open from 10:00 am - 12:00 pm and then again from 7:00 pm - 9:30 pm, and the Chinese restaurant was open from 11:00 am - 5:30 pm. Currently, it was 6:00 pm on a Tuesday so that left the bar as their only option for potential food.

The bar was a transformed pizza hut restaurant with a dimly lit interior, a pool table, a ping pong table with seemingly no paddles, and a large patio around the back that overlooked the ocean. The chairs were well worn but half decent and accompanied hand-crafted wood tables. The actual bar itself looked like the one from Stanley Kubrick's The Shining and gave Shelly the creeps. The bartender was cute, maybe twenty-two or twenty-three, he had curly blonde hair that had been cut into a mullet, one green and one brown eye, and a sleeve tattoo of some sort of movie scene that Shelly couldn't quite make out. His voice was higher than she imagined given his muscular physique but it still suited him

"Anywhere you'd like," he was drying glasses and placing them back on the bar before drying his hands and making his way to the table that had chosen with their menus.

"I'm Tom by the way, are you guys just visiting or?" He handed them the menus as he asked.

It was Cosmina who answered, "No, we actually just moved here, up by Fernwood."

"Oh! You're the new tattoo artist. Yeah, I've heard all about you. You met my cousin and my uncles last time you were out here. My cousin is probably around your age I'm assuming," He addressed Shelly now who had thrown herself full-heartedly into her menu.

"I've heard she's exactly my age actually."

"Sick, well we go fishing all the time if you ever want to join us. We'll stop by on our way next time, and see if you're up to it."

"Sure, why not."

He smiled at her and told them to let him know when they were ready to order. He seemed nice enough, maybe she could make some friends here. Get to know Tom and his cousin, and learn to fish.

They all ordered some variation of seafood which seemed risky given that it was a bar, all of which were surprisingly delicious considering their oversight of location. They chatted for a bit about how odd it felt to be out of the city and know they weren't just on vacation. Her mother commented on how charming the town was and her father agreed while claiming his year end goal was to have his work featured in the gallery that graced the main street. They talked about the kitchen and Cosmina's ideas for it, about whether or not they would keep the yard wild or turn a section into a small garden. Shelly talked about how wonderful Edward was and how happy she was that Jibbles didn't seem to mind him. The start of the day had sucked, but it was starting to turn around and Shelly had almost forgotten about seeing the boy in the woods again. After they had paid her parents both excused themselves to the washroom since her mother wasn't sure what the plumbing situation at her new shop would be.

The second they left Tom appeared.

"Hey, so uh, I didn't want to say anything around your parents 'cause they might think I'm crazy or something. But be careful if you go out into the woods alone."

"Well, yeah, I'm not trying to get eaten by wolves or something."

"Well.. yeah, that. But, there's something out there. Me and Sam, my cousin, we saw this thing a few years ago. It didn't look quite human and it definitely wasn't an animal. We didn't really stay out there long enough to find out. But it was right around there, and you seem like you might be someone who wanders into the woods, so-"

Shelly cut him off, "I seem like someone who wanders off into the woods? What's that mean?"

"I don't know. You just seem kind of lonely. I guess you just moved here so it makes sense. But you seem kind of empty."

"Well that's not a very nice thing to say to someone you just met. Thanks for the advice," Shelly slammed the napkin she had been wringing in her hands down onto the table and stormed towards the exit as her mother made her way out of the bathroom. Shelly didn't stop, simply walked right passed her and out onto the street.

"Hey, slow down, what's wrong."

"Is there something wrong with me or something?"

Aki had joined them outside, "whoa, what makes you say that? Did Tom say something to you?"

"Yah. He called me pathetic."

"He what!" Cosmina turned on her heel to storm back inside.

"Well," Shelly stopped her, "he didn't say pathetic. He just said I seem lonely like I'm empty or something. I don't know, sometimes I feel like he might be right."

Her mother let out a defeated sigh and pulled Shelly into her chest, "you're not empty, baby. You just need to try and stay positive all right? This is a fresh start. Nothing but good things are coming from now on. Okay?"

Shelly nodded her head and pulled away from her mother's hug of positivity, changing the subject by asking what direction the tattoo shop was in.

▪

That night Shelly paced the room as she dialled Sal's number. It rang, once, twice, three times, "hello?" Sal picked up.

Shelly bumped into a pile of boxes that had been stacked beside her bed when she heard Sal's voice. She steadied them before she spoke.

"Hey, you said to call you?"

Sal hesitated, crap, "I just thought we should talk about what happened today, what it meant. When you went chasing after Edward and we found you. You were crying and I just don't want you to feel like I pressured you or like you were just going along because you didn't know what to do or you regretted it or something. I wanted to make sure that you're okay. That we're okay. I don't want to lose you or our friendship, you mean so much to me and I think that maybe I'm in love with you. I mean obviously, I don't know since we don't even know what's going on and now I'm realizing maybe I shouldn't have said that cause that might put even more pressure on you. But I want you to know that that meant something to me. That you mean something to me and I can't wait to come and visit you so we can actually figure out what all of this is and what it means and-"

"Sal, it's okay. I wanted that. I want so much more with you too. I thought maybe I meant nothing to you and I've been worrying about it all day. I don't want to lose you either. Feeling you today... touching you .. that was .. I've been wanting that for a long time to, and I'm glad it happened."

"Oh thank god. I. And. See. when."

"Hello? Hello?"

"Hear. Me."

Shelly pulled her phone from her ear to see only one bar. She hopped up onto her bed and tried to connect to a stronger signal. The call dropped.

"Fuck."

She looked and Edward and Jibbles who had already made themselves comfortable. Jibbles was plopped onto the pillow she didn't use, ready to smother her in her sleep when she seemed a little too peaceful, and Edward lay at the end of her bed. He faced the door, ready to protect her from any danger and reminding her of the events of the day. She crawled into bed next to them and shut off her phone.

▪

The next day her parents had gone to town to spend some time at the tattoo shop, working on ideas for redesign, filling out forms and permits, seeing if any maintenance needed to be done, and hopefully bringing home some groceries. They had stopped and grabbed cereal, milk, and an oven-ready pizza on the way home from town the night before. But it was hardly noon and cereal only went so far, plus she didn't want to make the pizza in case they forgot to grab groceries on their way and then there was no dinner. On the bright side the wifi installment guy had shown up and they were now back to living in luxury with high speed. Her parents had also taken the time to set up the large furniture and mount the TV while Shelly slept this morning, so the house felt a little less empty and more so like home. However, it was hard not to notice the large gaps of space that were now between the couch and the recliner chair, and pretty much everything else besides the dining room set. Moving from an apartment with maximalist parents to a house where you didn't have enough furniture to fill the house felt odd. It was all of their things, and the place felt like home because of it, but she felt like a stranger here. Like any moment she might need to ask the host where the bathroom is again or figure out how to use a ridiculously made shower head. She did however find comfort in her pets, and the beauty of the place.

She could do without the white kitchen but knew that would be gone soon enough.

She had spent the morning unpacking her room, arranging and then rearranging. At first, she had set it up exactly how her old room had been, there was comfort in that too. But she kept hearing her mother's voice chiming about a fresh start and what that meant for them so she rearranged it into a setup she had never done before. She set up her desk on the wall to the right of her bed, her bookshelf sat beside that. She put her dresser on the wall opposite her bed and thought about getting a chair to put beside the window. She had never had this much space before and the thought of adding a reading chair made her feel uncharacteristically giddy.

When her room was done she made her way to the kitchen for her second bowl of cereal of the day. She gave Jibbles her leftover milk and got Edward a treat from the cupboard which he devoured instantly. She was scrolling through her phone when she thought she saw something run by her out of the corner of her eye. She froze and looked down at Edward who had stopped licking the floor for crumbs and now sat perfectly still, his ears raised. Even jibbles had stopped drinking his milk and now stared at the far corner of the house. A low growl started in Jibbles's stomach and the hackles on Edwards's back began to raise as he cautiously made his way to his feet.

Ding Dong.

Shelly jumped and placed her hand on her chest as the doorbell rang out a second time. Ding Dong. Jibbles had stopped growling and Edward was now back to normal and barking at the door. Shelly opened it to see Tom and a girl she could only assume was his cousin.

"Hey," Tom gave her a half smile and dropped his eyes at the look of annoyance on her face.

"I'm Sam," She ignored the tension in the air and stuck her hand out for Shelly to shake. She was on the taller side, maybe 5'6" - 5'7", definitely taller than herself and Sal. She had an afro

that was dyed blonde on one half and naturally dark on the other. She had an incredibly dark complexion that Shelly couldn't help but admire, even though she felt like she was slightly betraying Sal. Her lips were full, like Sal's, and her nose was triple pierced with gold hoops. She wore loose-fitting shorts that hung just above her knee and a tight crop top with a see-through rain jacket that showed off a tattoo of a bull skull on her chest.

Shelly shook her hand, "Shelly. Nice tattoo."

"Thanks," Sam held her hand a bit too long and Shelly pulled away, feeling awful that for a moment she had been so in awe of Sam she had forgotten all about Sal. She wondered if maybe Tom was right, she was empty and was trying to fill a void with beautiful people. Or maybe she thought that if she somehow was close to their confidence and filled herself with them and them with her that she would be able to absorb what she didn't have.

"Look," it was Tom who spoke next, "I wanted to come and apologize. I'm sorry I said you seemed empty, that wasn't my place."

"He gets ahead of himself sometimes, he really didn't mean any offence."

"It's okay, I overreacted a little. Yesterday was just... not easy."

"I hear ya," Sam moved passed Shelly and into the house.

Tom just shrugged when Shelly looked from her new intruder to the intruder apologist before motioning him to come inside as well.

"Aren't you a cutie Mr..."

"Edward."

"Mr. Edward," Sam scratched Edward's nose, scooped up Jibbles and rocked him in her arms as she wandered around the living room, "I moved here in my grade eight year. Fucking brutal. Not to mention I'm the only black kid on this entire island. By the way, it's great to see another beautiful woman of

colour around here," she winked at Shelly and Shelly bit the inside of her lip in response, "but anywho. It's not so bad once you get used to it. And if you liked the outdoors it's pretty cool, I go hiking a lot and I hear you're a photographer, so if you ever want someone to show you the sites, let me know. Oh, I also hear Tommy boy over here invited you to come fishing with us. And I know, it's like Ugggh fishing, who wants to do that? But we go out on the lake, sometimes the ocean, usually the lake though and in the summer we mostly just swim. There's just something about the water you know, there's a sort of," and the next words they said in unison, "comfort in it."

Sam's eyes lit up, "exactly! See Tom, I told you she'd be our friend."

"When the hell did she agree to that? You've just been talk talk talking," he mimicked a puppet with his hands and Sam rolled her eyes at his typical response to one of her many monologues.

"Sam seems cool, and Tom you're... here, I guess. And I need friends anyway. So fuck it."

"Everyone just hates on Tom," he shook his head and sat down crosslegged to pet Edward and Jibbles who had recently jumped out of Sam's arms.

"Cause you're a preppy white boy, you're easy to hate. Right, Shelly?"

Shelly felt looser now, more willing to accept Sam's confidence as her own and leaned into the joke and the possibility of new friends, a new start.

"Sorry Tom, but she's right. Whose opening line of friendship is do you want to go fishing? Only a white boy says shit like that." The ironic thing was she actually loved to fish. Dip netting had been a vital part of her trips north to visit her grandparents. But this was not traditional fishing the way her family had done it, this was rich white person with high tech gear and a speed boat fishing so she felt it fair to make the jab at Tom anyways.

Tom hung his head in defeat and stood up, walking to the door.

"This is embarrassing then," he said as he pulled the door open, "we're heading out fishing... want to come?"

Shelly said she couldn't retract her further statement but that she did in fact want to go and asked them to wait while she went to change.

They waited at the door while Shelly ran downstairs to her room and Sam took it upon herself to get Edward ready. She grabbed his collar and leash that hung on the coat rack beside the door and leashed him up.

"For the first time in a long time, I'm excited Tom. There's just something about her like she knows somehow."

"What the hell are you talking about?"

"The forest, whatever's out there. I get this feeling that she knows something about it, that the reason she got so mad at you is because you spooked her and she was trying not to let on. You can't tell me that part of you didn't think about that when you told her that we saw something out there. You've met tons of people that come out here in the summer and not once have you ever mentioned that they need to be careful or even told them not to go out there alone. You've literally helped backpackers find the trails to hike out and acted like you had no idea they might not come back. Part of me thought you had forgotten all about it."

"So?"

"So! So what? Are you serious Tom? Why else would you have mentioned it to her?"

"I don't know. She seemed so alone. And the only time we ever saw it was when we felt that way too."

Sam's defensiveness at his meagre so dissipated and she stepped back, crossing her arms.

"I never said anything about feeling alone. I had you didn't I? I'd say that's the exact opposite of feeling alone."

"Sam. We both know a person can be completely alone even when they're surrounded by people. Think about it. That was the year my dad died and I'm so grateful to Kiyana for letting me stay with her. She didn't have to do that, I'd only lived with her for three years. Don't get me wrong I love your aunt and she never made me feel isolated or alone or anything like that, but I still felt that way without him. And that's the year he who won't be named stole all that money from you. You can't tell me you lost your boyfriend and best friend in one go and didn't feel like you had no one?"

Sam knew it was true but she didn't want Tom to think he hadn't done enough for her, "I had you.."

"Sure, we had each other and I've always loved our adventures and stuff. But two broken and empty people can't fill each other up when they don't have anything to give Sam. And just like how you're sure that Shelly knows something. I'm sure that she's empty like we used to be..." he trailed off for a moment, "like we still are."

"What's with the solemn mood all of a sudden?" Shelly was rounding the top of the stairs and could feel an odd tension strung out between the cousins.

Sam forced herself not to look and Tom and threw a smile across her face, "Nothing. Tom was just wanting to go take the boat out on the ocean and I think we should take you down to the lake. Right, Tom?"

He threw his arms up and silently asked Shelly what can ya do?

▪

The crew made their way to the end of the driveway where Tom had parked his pickup truck on the side of the road. Claiming they didn't want to drive up with the boat in case there wasn't enough space to turn around. Shelly figured they didn't want to drive up with the boat in case she realized it was them and didn't answer the door.

Sam still had Edward, he didn't walk as well for her and pulled on his leash whenever something caught his eye or a new scent found its way to him. Sam hadn't minded though. She simply let him do what he wanted and only stopped following his lead when he tried to leave the driveway. When they reached the pickup Sam let Edward sit in the front seat with Tom and squished into the back with Shelly and all of their gear.

"You're officially part of the crew now Shelly. How does it feel?" Tom looked back at her through the rearview mirror.

She joked back, "fulfilling," and she wished she had been able to fully mean it.

Chapter 6

the cowboy

The past few months had gone by just like her mother had said. No heebie jeebies, no more shadows or little boys and girls in the woods. It was a fresh start and Shelly was convinced that she had been tricking herself into thinking the things that had scared her in the city had followed her here.

She had spent her time fishing with Tom and Sam, hiking with Sam and Edward and occasionally jibbles if he would get in the backpack, watching movies with Sam, going to the beach for sunset drinks with Sam and sometimes Tom, and hanging out with Sam and her dads. They had grown exceptionally close over the five months since Shelly had moved, and when Sal and Kyra had to cancel their trip last minute due to storm warnings, they had grown even closer. Shelly had been a mess and Sam took it upon herself to spend the entire break with her. They shared a bed every night, and sometimes Shelly would wake up to Sam's hand draped across her belly beneath her shirt. The first few times she moved it, thinking of Sal and what they might have, but after a week she left it, snuggling in closer to the warmth of Sam's body.

They liked to talk, no matter what they did they always talked. At first, it was surface-level things, what they were planning to do in school after their year off, what their parents embarrassing nicknames for them had been, what they thought they wanted to be when they grew up back in the seven grade, their favourite type of weather or books or movies. And then it started to get deeper, Sam told Shelly about her ex-boyfriend and how he had stolen all the money from her savings account and cheated on her with her best friend, how she had always thought she liked women but wasn't sure until she met her ex-girlfriend, who ended up moving to Paris and fell in love with some older French woman. Shelly thought her life sounded like a great greek tragedy, losing her money and lover and best friend, losing the woman she thought was the love of her life to a French woman fifteen years their senior who offered her fame and money and a luxurious life. She told Shelly how her name used to be Samuel and she didn't want to go through all the hassle of being dead named so she just stuck to the shortened version, and called herself Sam. She said people had an easier time calling her that since they had always known her by that name anyways. Then Shelly told her about Sal, how she didn't what they were, if they were. How Sal had told her they thought they might love her and followed it up with nothing but the friendship they had always had. Sam had reassured her that she was incredible and anyone would be lucky to be with her. She had brushed the hair that stuck to her forehead with sweat from her brow as she told her how beautiful she thought she was. She told her that she was sure Sal was just scared to lose their friendship and probably did love her, that she was a comet that lit up the night sky whenever there was darkness and the light she brought filled the air with specs of gold. Shelly had thought those seemed more like her feelings than Sal's, and Sam had meant it that way but never said so. Then Shelly had told her about the shadows, about the things she saw from the corners of her eye, and Sam told her she had seen similar things, like the one she and Tom saw in the woods, the one Tom had warned her about.

It was during that talk, about the thing in the woods that Edward's hackles stood up for the first time since the day they had first met Sam. Shelly and Sam fell silent. They didn't know why, but they both had the sudden urge to lay flat on their stomachs and hide behind the log they had been sitting on. Shelly held her finger to her lips and looked at Edward, her eyes pleading with him to be silent. They moved slowly, trying to preserve the silence that had fallen over the forest and laid as flat as they could behind the log. Shelly motioned for

Edward to lie down as well and he did. He whimpered as she patted his head to calm him and she held her fingers to her lips once more. They breathed as quietly as they could and didn't dare to do more, not even swallow the spit that had begun accumulating in their mouths.

A twig snapped on the other side of the log and Sam threw her hand over her mouth to stop from screaming. Another snap, this one sounded larger, almost as though a whole branch had been snapped from the trees. Then it was silent again.

Minutes passed, ten, twenty, they laid still. Then another snap, farther away this time. Then the yipping started. It was the same as the sounds from her dream the night she had noticed it was a mirror. The yips turned to cackles and were soon accompanied by a shriek that felt as though it were fracturing their bones. The shriek turned into a wailing, painful sound, as though an animal had been turned inside of itself and made to call a melody to the woods. Tears streamed down the girl's faces and Edward flattened his ears, all of their eyes clenched shut, afraid of what they might see if it came back.

The woods fell silent again, save for the few leaves that crunched every so often under the soft tread of something smaller, not capable of snapping a large branch like whatever it was that had been there before.

Edward's head lifted from the ground and his ears perked up. He stuck his nose in the air and sniffed frantically, trying to decipher the direction the thing was coming from. But the woods were all skewed, the air wasn't right and the wind seemed to swirl in every direction. Even the sounds of the leaves seemed like they were coming from all around them. One moment a crunch could be heard from the right, the next it was coming from in front of them, and the next moment from the left.

Edward nudged at Shelly, and when she didn't move or open her eyes he nudged harder. She opened her eyes and held her finger to her lips again, urging Edward to stop. He nudged her again, fear in his eyes. He seemed to be pleading with her to move, to get out of the woods NOW. She finally understood and gently shook Sam whose eyes flew up and met Shelly's with pure terror. She hadn't even seemed human in that instant, and Shelly thought about what

Tom had said, that there was something out here and they had seen it and she now realized just how wrong the thing must have seemed to make Sam so afraid. The girl whose confidence Shelly wished she could drink up endlessly was scared beyond belief. She nodded her head towards the log, motioning that they needed to go. Sam shook her head wildly, unblinking as her eyes refused to leave Shelly's face. Shelly pointed to Edward who nudged at her again, frantically this time. She looked at Sam again, grabbing her hand and squeezing it to let her know they wouldn't leave her behind. Sam took a shakey breath and covered her face when it came out too loud. Shelly nodded to let her know it was okay and pressed her fingers to her lips one last time then pointed to the log again, or more so through the log, to the place they had come from.

The two of them began to move into a crouch, with Edward keeping low as if getting ready to stalk prey. They scanned the forest and saw nothing. Then something shook the ferns to their right and Edward swung his head in the direction of the movement, following with his eyes as whatever it was made its way in behind them in a large half circle. They stood taller now, still keeping quiet as they stepped carefully over the log. Edward had pinned his ears back and sent his hackles as high as they could go. Shelly found him quite scary to look at this way and was glad he was so loyal to her.

Then it happened, her phone lit up in her pocket and began to buzz, then ring. It sent shock waves through the forest and froze the trio in place. Then the ferns behind them parted and it was the same as the dream she had had all those months ago.

Three coyotes had emerged from the ferns, their fur tattered and ripped in places that shouldn't have been possible. One's whole face consisted of only bone, another's front ribs were exposed, the third's spine pushed up in a jagged column and broke through the raw hide. Their claws were longer than they should have been and blackened blood dripped from their jaws. Shelly staggered back and heard a crunch beneath her feet. She looked down and saw bone. The snap they had heard hadn't been a large branch, it had been a skull snapping in half, ripped from its body. The body that lay half a foot to the left had been ripped to tatters save for one arm that bored the same sleeve tattoo as Tom's. Sam gasped and gagged as she recognize the blonde curls on the severed head.

The coyotes howled and began their cackling yip once more.

"Run!" Shelly shouted as she tugged at Sam's arm and they took off through the woods.

Edward flanked them, keeping pace and pushing them forward, forcing them not to stop when the breath started to leave their lungs too quickly and fill them too slowly. Tears had begun to fill their eyes again and blurred their vision. Shelly stepped on a rock that shifted under her weight and pulled her ankle in a direction it shouldn't go. She yelled in pain but didn't stop. She knew she had to keep running, knew they wouldn't stop until they were free of the forest, and wasn't sure they would even stop then. Sam had begun to fall behind and Shelly yelled at her to keep running, that they were going to make it. Sam kept repeating Tom's name, over and over, losing her breath to the wail of pain that escaped in the name of her cousin. The edge of the forest was visible now and Shelly felt her legs picking up their pace. She pushed forward. Edward yelped behind her and she turned her head to see one of the coyotes, if they could even be called that, had tackled him to the ground. They were rolling one on top of the other, their jaws snapping at the other as claws dug into their sides. Edward yelped again as the coyote bit down on his shoulder. But he was bigger, and Shelly had to hope he would make it out without her. The other two were gaining on her and Sam and they couldn't keep up their pace much longer.

They burst through the trees and stumbled as their feet dropped and their knees jammed into themselves. They scrambled out of the ditch and onto the road, not stopping when their feet hit the pavement. They ran until they no longer could and collapsed onto the burning asphalt in the mid-day sun. They curled in on themselves and sobbed, sobbed for each other, for Tom, for Edward. They clung to the hope that Edward would make it out, that he could somehow take all of them. They sobbed at the fact that Shelly had been right and those things hadn't followed them out of the forest. They sobbed at the remembrance of the shriek they had heard. Then their heads shot up as they heard a gargled whimper coming from the ditch. They shot to their feet, forcing their legs not to give out from beneath them. Then Edward staggered over the incline and collapsed on the edge of the road. Shelly ran to him and tried to pick him up without hurting him further. He whimpered at the clumsy way she tried to balance his weight. Sam moved to the other side of him, helping Shelly to balance him out. He lay stretched between the two of them, breathing in short bursts that made him shudder as the holes in his side gushed blood.

They heard the sound of a pickup truck coming up the road and made their way quickly toward it. As it rounded the corner they could see it was Tom's truck. They shot each other and look and backed slowly to the edge of the road, unsure of who or what they would see.

Tom slammed the brakes when he saw the two of them and Edward covered in blood and hardly breathing. He jumped out of the truck and through the back door open before running over to them. He took Edward from their arms and rushed him to the truck. They stood unmoving, staring at him as he hopped back in the driver's seat. He threw the truck in reverse and spun it around wildly.

"What the fuck are you waiting for get in!"

Shelly and Sam scrambled up the back and into the box, too afraid to get in the vehicle next to the man whose head had only moments before been severed from the rest of him. They shook, their bodies going into shock as Tom flew down the highway and into town. The vet clinic was on the other side of town, normally a forty-minute drive from the end of the road where Sam and Shelly's houses sat. Tom made it there in fifteen. Shelly and Sam stayed seated in the box as Tom picked up Edward and ran through the open door of the vet clinic. They didn't know how long he had been gone and they didn't care. They were numb and the only thing Shelly could think about was Edward, how he might be okay if she had listened to him on his first warning, how the last thing he might have experienced was her abandoning him. She put her head between her knees and rocked back and forth until Tom came back out.

"Edward's in surgery, they're going to call me when they know more. I'm sorry Shelly but they don't know if he'll make it." Shelly didn't look at him, just kept rocking back and forth. Sam stared at him blankly and the way her eyes seemed to be made of lifeless glass made his skin crawl.

"They're going to try though. I told them I'd pay for whatever he needed," he added after a moment touching Shelly's shoulder.

She winced and he quickly pulled away.

"Look, I don't know what happened. And you guys don't have to get into the truck. But I need to take you to the hospital all right?"

The girls continued their silence and Tom took that as an okay. He disappeared inside the cab for a moment before coming back with a blanket. He haphazardly wrapped it around their shoulders then made his way back to the driver's seat and drove them to the hospital.

▪

The hospital was small, less intimidating than the ones Shelly had been to when she lived in the city. The shock had begun to wear off her more so than it had Sam who was still wrapped in the blanket with Tom guiding her toward the door to emergency. Shelly walked behind them and looked in the window as they passed through the automatic doors. No wonder Tom had wanted them to bring them here. They were covered in cuts and scratches from head to toe, some large enough that they had both leaked a decent amount of blood over themselves. Shelly noticed broken-off twigs tangled into the back of Sam's hair and figured hers must look similar to that as well given the matted look it had in the window reflection. Her ankle hurt with every step and by the time they had made it through the doors she could barely stand on it. It had swollen to triple the size of what it should have been and was starting to discolour with blue and purple bruises. She snorted as she thought of the irony that part of her looked like the boy from the woods that she was so scared of and how he didn't seem all that scary anymore. Sure, he made her uneasy and she knew he was out there somewhere, and so was Hannah. But she found an odd sort of comfort in knowing that, what she didn't find comforting in the least was the shrieking wail from the woods or the fact that her dream hadn't been a simple nightmare. Of course, she knew that there was more to it than that, but her grandmother had always talked about the way a person could interpret a dream and assumed it was something to be interpreted, not something to heed with caution.

The nurses dropped what they had been doing the instant they saw the three of them and rushed over a wheelchair for Shelly to sit in, and a second one for Sam. As they were being wheeled away and into the blinding fluorescent hallway that for some reason they felt the need to paint in all white so a person felt as though they were ascending into heaven when they went into it, a nurse defensively approached Tom and began questioning him while another dialled the police.

By the time the police arrived Sam had been bandaged and cleared of any potential brain or internal injuries. She was suffering from shock which had been clear to Tom the moment he saw her but was beginning to snap out of it, and the doctor felt confident she would be able to speak to the police soon. Shelly was still in the back wing of the hospital and had been waiting on the results of an X-Ray that had been taken before anything else had been done. A nurse was in the process of bandaging her newly cleaned wounds when the doctor informed her that her ankle had suffered something called a lateral malleolus fracture, which the doctor translated as a fibula-only fracture. She told her that she would be able to walk on it as long as she wore a boot once the swelling had gone down, but should try and stay on crutches or in a wheelchair for at least a few weeks to help it heal faster. Shelly agreed to the crutches and was given a pair once she had joined the others in the waiting room.

Both of her parents, as well as Sam's, were now there as well. Marcus and Izac, Sam's dads were talking in a hushed tone with Tom near the far end of the waiting room. Marcus was panicked and seemed angry at Tom for some reason. Izac kept glancing toward Sam who still refused to speak or look up from the floor. When the doctor wheeled Shelly over Sam's eyes finally stopped searching the speckled linoleum beneath her feet. She had more bandages and large bandages than Shelly had. But aside from those and the matted hair, Shelly thought she looked better than Sam did. Tom held his hand up to his uncles for a moment and made his way over to Shelly whose parents had begun their interrogation of the doctor and Shelly's nurses.

"Hey," Tom bent down beside her and touched her arm, "I got a call from the vet when you were in there. They said Ed's gonna make it."

Shelly stared at him for a moment before her eyes filled with tears and she flung her arms around his neck.

"Thank you," she sobbed into his shoulder as Sam got up and threw her arms around the two of them and began to cry as well.

It felt odd to hug him. She had half expected him to be cold and lifeless, or to disappear into thin air like a thick fog the second her arms made contact with him. But he was really there, and alive. His body was warm to the touch and his breath was hot on her back. His arms felt strong wrapped around the two of them, and then Shelly felt her own shirt beginning to soak through with hot tears as well.

Tom wasn't sure why he was crying, but he couldn't stop the tears from coming so he let them fall as he held tightly to his friend and his cousin. They were all he had and he didn't know why in those few moments they had seemed so scared of him.

Someone cleared their throat behind them and the three broke apart, wiping their eyes and looking towards the policeman who had finished consulting with the nurses who had helped them when they first arrived.

"I need to speak with you all," then he addressed Sam, "if you're able to."

Sam nodded and said she could speak.

"Okay. Come with me please," they all moved to follow him into the office behind the check-in desk, he stopped and turned to Tom, "not you son. I would like to speak with you privately."

Sam and Shelly shot a worried glance at Tom who assured them it was fine and he had nothing to hide.

Aside from the fact you were just fucking decapitated Shelly thought as Sam wheeled her into the back room.

The officer sat across from them, in the doctor's chair while they sat in the chairs of the people who are told without an ounce of true empathy that their family member, their friend, they, weren't going to make it.

"Okay girls, I need you to tell me what happened to you," he turned to Shelly, "and your dog. And what Tom out there had to do with it."

"Tom didn't do anything," they both assured him to which he answered that Tom seemed to do an awful lot including driving like a maniac through town with two beat-up girls in the box of his pickup.

"We were out hiking in the woods, the ones that come off of Langs Road," Sam started, she was the better liar of the two so Shelly had let her take the lead, "you know there's that small trail out there?"

"Yeah, I know the trail," The cop chewed on the end of a toothpick as he talked to them.

Shelly had seen him around town every now and then and occasionally he stopped in to question her mother about some of her customers and sometimes he was a customer himself. He was a well-built man, but not very tall. Only a couple of inches above Sam. He kept his hair buzzed like he had once been a military man so Shelly had always assumed he'd be like one in demeanour as well. But he wasn't. He listened to them intently and assured them he didn't think that Tom had done anything wrong when they assured him again that he hadn't, that he was just following proper procedure so they didn't need to worry. Shelly didn't like cops, they made her uneasy, and she could tell they made Sam uneasy too. Still, she appreciated that he was kind to them and hadn't acted as though somehow their injuries were their fault.

Sam continued her version of the truth and said that they had been hiking and run across a mama bear and her cubs on their way back down the trail, that they usually put a bear bell on Edwards's collar but they had forgotten. She told him how they had gotten spooked and didn't want to cause any problems with the bear so they decided to cut through the forest and make a loop around it. That's when they had run into the pack of coyotes that attacked Edward. They were skinny she said and looked like they had been struggling to find food. The cop had raised his eyebrows at this, struggling to find food in the winter made sense, but not at this time of year, when spring was almost over and there was plenty of wildlife in the forest. Still, Sam insisted that's what they had looked like, and in a way, she wasn't lying. They had looked like they were starving, albeit they looked like they were dead, but there wasn't a whole lot of difference between the two. Then Sam told him that the coyotes had chased them, that Edward had hung back to fight them off once they got too close, that Sam had tripped while they were running and that's what had happened to her ankle, that they were scared and didn't notice the branches grabbing at them and ripping their skin open because they were so full of adrenaline. She told him how they had collapsed on the road and Edward had come limping out after them and that was when Tom showed up.

She had told Shelly once that the trick to a good lie was to tell the truth and omit certain parts of it, rather than making up a whole new story. That way it was harder to forget what the lie actually was and much harder to get caught. She felt like they were in the clear. The cop seemed to believe them and didn't seem to have any more questions. He had closed his notebook and looked ready to dismiss them before he flipped it back open and looked back up at them.

"Why didn't they follow you?"

"What?"

"The coyotes, why didn't they follow you?"

"We don't know," it was Shelly who spoke now. She thought it was suspicious if she didn't contribute to the story, "we think maybe Edward scared them off. He's a pretty big

dog and maybe they realized it wasn't worth it. Or maybe they were scared to come out of the trees. We aren't really sure."

"Mhmm," he wrote something on his notepad, "so why was Tom up there though?"

Sam and Shelly looked at each other, they didn't have an answer for that.

"We don't know," Sam finally said.

Shelly added, "we're just glad he showed up. I wouldn't have a dog anymore if it weren't for him."

The cop seemed satisfied with that and Shelly was glad he didn't have any more questions. Sam wheeled Shelly out of the room and told Tom he was up.

He was in with the cop for about thirty minutes. Twenty longer than anyone expected him to be. When he finally came out he looked tired, and the cop seemed pleased enough to let everyone leave. He told them he would follow up should anything more come up, and to call him if they saw the coyotes again so he could call animal control.

Tom left the hospital first while Sam and Shelly's parents chatted about what had happened and what they should do. If they should call animal control themselves, ban the girls from going back into the woods, put up some kind of fence to keep them from coming too close to their houses? Shelly and Sam sat in silence. They had watched Tom drive away, both of them still wondering if it was really him and if it was what had they seen in the woods. The wounds on Edward had been real, so clearly, the coyotes had been too, but wouldn't that mean that the body had to be as well?

▪

When Shelly and her parents arrived at the vet clinic the assistant who ran the front desk informed them that the young man who had dropped Edward off had already stopped by and paid for all of his vet bills. Shelly's parents gave each other a look, thanked the woman, and went to collect Edward from the back where he had been resting. He struggled to his feet when he saw them. He had been completely shaved to get to his wounds. His side was stitched up and wrapped in bandages, as was his shoulder, and his front right leg. His snout had also been sewn up but no bandage was on it. He wore a cone around his neck and the vet informed them that it should be kept on for at least two months and they should bring him back in a couple of weeks for a check-up. He gave them some antibiotics he said were fine to put in some cheese or soft treats and a topical cream to rub gently into the sutures on his face. Shelly leaned on her crutches and kissed his nose when she saw him and whispered to him that she was sorry for leaving him and that he was a good dog. His tail wagged when she said it and she knew there was no feeling of abandonment on his part, but she couldn't shake the feeling of guilt.

▪

They arrived home well into the evening. The sun was still lighting up the sky as it always did when the summer months came, but Shelly and her parents were exhausted.

Edward hadn't been able to make it down the stairs to her room and neither had Shelly so she asked her father to bring her blankets to the living room and she made a bed beside Edward's on the floor. Jibbles curled up next to Edward's head instead of hers and they all drifted off to sleep.

▪

The dream began again as it always did. The cowboy with the hole in his chest rode to her on his horse. He dismounted, crushed his cigar with his boot, and his spur rang out. It was all the same as it had been and that made Shelly nervous. Even more so when she realized that Edward wasn't there this time. She turned around to check behind her. The world was still a mirror, she was still trapped in a never-ending desert that would loop back on itself at one point or another. But then, instead of motioning for Shelly to come to him. He stepped back, opening his body towards his horse, making a path for her to get on. She did. She made her way to the horse, grabbed the horn and stuck her foot in the stirrup and pulled herself into the saddled. Then, instinctively she removed her foot for the cowboy to pull himself up behind her to sit on the hind quarters of his horse. She looked around for Edward as the cowboy followed the motions she had just done and swung himself up behind the saddle. She hadn't ever really looked at the horse for that long, she was always more focused on the cowboy. But it was beautiful. It stood roughly sixteen hands high and was on the slimmer side, meant for running. He was a light-coloured paint with an all-white face and clouded blue eyes. His tail had been braided and just above his hip was a red handprint made from the dirt of the plateaus.

His gruff voice startled her when he said as softly as a man who had smoked cigars and breathed in sand all his life could, "he ain't comin' lil' lady. Too sore from today's tussle."

Shelly just nodded, she understood that this was a dream, but it was also real in its own way. She could feel the cold of the dead cowboy moving off of his body and clinging to the heat hers radiated. He kicked his horse up and told her when to move the reins and in which direction. They rode for hours, making their way up a steep incline of red rocks. He finally told her to pull back gently and let out a friendly "wooooah" to tell his horse to stop. It did and the two dismounted. The cowboy first, then Shelly. They were halfway up the side of a large hill that lead to one of the plateaus Shelly had seen far in the distance. The cowboy lead her and his horse into a small cave near the edge of where they stood. She looked around and saw that there was a fire pit made of stones arranged neatly in the cave's center and a pile of wood was stacked in the back corner. She watched as the cowboy built a fire, then pulled a small bundle of sage from a leather pouch that hung from the horn of his saddle.

He beckoned her to sit beside him, "sindah."

Shelly just looked at him, unsure of what he had said.

"It means sit down in your mother tongue."

"You speak Tsilhqot'in?"

"I do."

"Then why are you in the desert?"

The cowboy sighed and tilted his head towards the seat he had wished Shelly to sit in. She obliged and crossed her legs in the same fashion as the man beside her. He removed his hat and placed the edge of the sage into the fire, blowing on the flames as he removed it to coax more smoke out of the plant. He handed the bundle to Shelly and bent his head foreword, scooping the sages smoke up and over the back of his head. He repeated this several times before taking the sage and motioning for Shelly to do the same. She copied the moves as he done them and waited for him to answer he. All he said was, "it is important to smudge yourself, especially in times such as these."

She repeated her question, "Why are you in the desert?"

"Deni tsin nadint'i, a persons spirit is powerful.

She waited for an explanation.

"Your grandmother sent me here. To watch over you, as I watched over your mother. But you couldn't see me lil lady," he pointed to fingers at her eyes, then at himself and he closed his eyes as he pulled his fingers back into his closed fist, "you're eyes're closed. So I found you here instead."

"My grandmother sent you? Why."

"She knew they were slippin' away. Those day walkin' nightmares of hers. They were comin' for you and your mama, so she sent me to help you. Only problem was your ma', she wouldn't listen to me. I tried to show her, but she wouldn't have it. She shuts out all the bad things and runs from the ones she can't. But there's no out runnin' 'em. They'll follow you where'vre you go. You know that, so I don't have ta tell ya. I tried to warn you, that night with the dog. You're mind wasn't as open then. I couldn't say as much as'l needed to say. For that I'm sorry."

"How are you supposed to help me if you're not actually here, or there, in the real world, with me.

"I can't tell ya that. You have'ta figure that one out then come find me."

Shelly could feel the dream pulling away and tried to hold onto it, but she was waking up. She couldn't speak and she was starting to panic. She had so many more questions that would go unanswered and she worried she would never see him again.

He smiled at her and held her hand, "gwaxezintan, be careful."

Chapter 7

closing thoughts

Shelly woke up to the sunlight peaking through the curtains and the smell of bannok in the kitchen. She breathed it in so the scent filled her whole body and repeated the cowboys words to herself deni tsin nadint'i, qwaxezintan.

She ate her bannok with a spread of strawberry jam, got dressed, and applied Edward'c cream to his nose. He laid his head in her lap as she did it and fell asleep as she stroked his head between his eyes with her thumb the way her grandmother did when she was sick as a little kid.

There was a knock at the door and her mother told her she'd get it. She had decided to stay home to be with Shelly for the week while she and Edward got back on their feet. In reality it was just as much for Cosmina's peace of mind as it was for Shelly's and she had become curious about Tom's relationship to her daughter. That was who she had expected to see when she opened the door. Instead, Sal and Kyra stood on the front step, pillows and luggage in hand.

"We're sorry we didn't call first. But when you told us Shelly was in the hospital we freaked out and got here as fast as we could," Kyra hugged Cosmina as she spoke and they were invited inside.

"Sal?! Kyra! What the hell!"

"Hey!" They both dropped their bags beside the black brick wall and ran to Shelly and Edward on the floor.

They hugged for a long time before pulling away and asking to hear to the story. Shelly told them what Sam had told the cops and noticed that Sal always seemed to be uneasy in their seat when Sam was mentioned. Shelly hadn't meant to but she mainly addressed Kyra as she spoke and realized an ugly sort of feeling inside of her whenever she looked at Sal. Not that she wasn't happy Sal was there, she was, but how could they sit there and seem jealous of Sam when they hadn't mentioned anything about being in love with Shelly or even feeling anything for Shelly since the night she first moved. She assumed they had moved on, and not that she had, but Sal didn't get to be uncomfortable at the potential of someone new in her life when Sal had hardly bothered to be in it in anyway that was different than before.

Cosmina grabbed her jacket and said she was going to run some errands then stepped outside to see Tom's truck pulling up. So he was coming to check on her. She smiled and waved at him as she got into her own car and headed towards town.

Tom let himself in and kocked on the inside of the door as he did so. Edward's ears perked up and he lifted his head as Tom walked into the room.

"Hey, uh, I'm sorry I didn't realize you had company."

He stood awkwardly by her friends bags, holding a lemon mirangue pie, Shelly's favourite, "my uh, mom made you this."

"Tell her thanks, you can just put it in the kitchen. And it's totally fine you can stay."

Tom put the pie away and came back into the living room, snuggling up to Edward and inspecting him to make sure the vet hadn't missed anything. Shelly introduced him to her friends and asked him how Sam was doing.

He shook his head, "I don't know. She won't talk to me, won't even look at me. I don't know whats wrong. I tried to stop in before I came here and when I went into her room and she saw it was me she hid under her sheets, like I was some kind of ghost or something. She looked like a little kid. I know you guys were in the woods, did you-" He stopped himself when he remembered Shelly's friends.

Sal and Kyra looked at each other then announced they were going to grab a few more things from the car that they had brought over.

When Shelly heard the door close she told Tom there was more to the story than what they told the cop and she would explain it later when they had more time. That he should stay away from Sam for awhile and she'd let him know when her friends were gone and he could come back over to talk. He didn't say anything back to her, just told Edward he was a good boy, gave jibbles, who had refused to leave Edward's side, a scratch on the head, and told Shelly to let him know. He opened the door as Kyra and Sal came back in holding two stuffed animals and a toy mouse. They exchanged goodbyes and nice to meet you's then Tom left and Shelly's friends were back in the living room.

"One for each of you," Kyra said as they handed a large stuffed bear to Edward, a stuffed seal to Shelly and the toy mouse to Jibbles.

"So, we've only got a couple of days, and we know you're on crutches but we're going to make the best of it! What do you want to do? And Sal why are you being so quiet?"

"I'm just tired."

Sal was never "just tired" and they all knew that, but Kyra could sense the tension so left it and didn't say anything more.

They settled on a movie marathon. Kyra suggested horror movies to which Shelly practically yelled no.

"Jeez, I thought you liked horror movies."

"I did. I do, just not right now."

They didn't argue with her. They collectively decided that Disney movies were their best bet, nostalgia was always good for the soul her mother would say, missing the old was a good thing.

"Snacks. We need snacks. Sal why don't you wait with Shelly and I'll run to town real quick and get some."

Shelly protested and said she would just text her mom but Kyra insisted that she go with the rational that they had no idea what time she would be back. And with that she was out the door, and Sal and Shelly were alone.

"So.."

"So.."

"I've missed you."

"Have you? Cause you've hardly called, and you haven't acknowledged what's going on once since I moved here."

Sal wrung their shirt tail in their hands. Shelly hadn't even noticed that Sal didn't bother with the nipple covers today. That would explain why Tom was so awkward when he showed up.

"Can we talk in your room or something? I don't like feeling so exposed."

Sal helped Shelly down the stairs and they sat side by side on the edge of her bed.

"I meant what I said. But I didn't know what to do, and you didn't make any moves to acknolwdge it either, so I left it. Then you started talking to us about this Sam person and posting pictures of the two of you out hiking and walking Edward and stuff and I thought maybe you were with her and that's why you left it."

"Are you serious?" The ugly feeling had come back and was suddenly bubbling up in Shelly's stomach, she wanted to hold it back but it started to spew out of her, "YOU told ME you were in love with me."

"Maybe.."

"Maybe! Whatever! YOU kissed ME before I left. YOU started touching ME in the woods. And yeah, I liked it, I wanted it, I still want it. I still want you, but you left me high and dry. You hardly talked to me other than texts in the group chat. But just you and me? It was like I didn't even exist! I thought maybe I loved you to, maybe we had something, maybe we were something but we don't really click do we?"

Sal looked like Shelly had slapped them across the face and her anger quickly subsided.

Now it was Sal's turn to be angry, "We don't click! Then why the fuck have we been friends for ten years, just for shits and fucking giggles!?" They were standing now, facing Shelly who couldn't do much but sit there and take it.

"Maybe we don't click because you're too fucking scared to tell your parents your gay! Ever thought of that?! Maybe. Just MAYBE I didn't know what to do because you haven't even bothered to tell your mom you don't like cock."

They were breathing heavily and their throat hurt from screaming at Shelly. Sal instantly regretted bringing up Shelly's parents, it was something they had talked about countless times and it hadn't been fair of them to throw that in her face. They sat down and hung their head, avoiding Shelly's eyes that had begun to glass over.

Their voice was small when they spoke again, "I'm sorry. That wasn't fair. You mean a lot to me. And I have really missed you. I'd really like to try and make something work. If you want to to? And we can take things slow, we don't have to rush anything. I know were already close but I think we should really try and build something strong, learn to be more vulnerable in a different way. You know?"

Shelly blinked away the tears that had been forming in her eyes and grabbed Sal's hand, "I'd like that."

"Okay," Sal was beaming at her, and Shelly felt something in her stomach drop, "and we should think about telling your parents if you're ready."

Shelly leaned over and kissed them, "I am."

Then she looked back at the door that still stood slightly open and then glanced down at Sal's chest, "You know, town's fairly far away. I bet she won't be back for another forty minutes or so."

"Oh really," Sal cocked an eye brow at Shelly.

Shelly shimmied out of the dress she had been wearing since pants were difficult to put on over her boot and she didn't want to take it off. Sal whistled at the bright pink thong and lack of bra that Shelly had on. They took off their own clothes and crawled on top of Shelly pushing their knee between her thighs while they made out. Shelly slipped her hand between the two of them and Sal grinded up against it. They began kissing Shelly's neck, making their way to her chest. Shelly moaned as Sal gently bit at her boobs and traced her hand over Shelly's hip and along her waistline, making her shiver. Sal continued down, trailing her tongue along Shelly's abdomen and biting softly at each hip bone. They pushed Shelly's legs apart, stopping to ask if Shelly was sure she wanted this, she said yes and wrapped her good leg around Sal's neck, pulling them into her. Sal's tongue flicked and Shelly pulled their head closer, grinding to the motion of Sal's tongue. She moaned and Sal gripped her hips, pulling the two of them even closer. Shelly started to feel hot, and the heat rushed through her. She arched her back and her legs shook in voluntarily.

She moaned again this time louder, "oh yes Sam."

Sal stopped.

"What did you just say?"

Shelly sat up, "What."

"You just called me fucking SAM!"

"No I didn't. I said Sal."

"Unbelievable. You agree to be my girlfriend, decide you want me to make you cum and as soon as you get what you want from me you call out some random chicks name while my face is between your legs. I can't believe I thought I might actually love you. You're just using me."

Shelly scrambled to pull the blankets over her as Sal got dressed and headed for the door.

"Sal. Please stop, I love you. You just have similar names and she's the only person I hangout with here."

"Oh yeah? Well what about Tom? You want to go again and call out Tom's name this time?" Sal scoffed, "and just for the record. I don't think you know what love is. You're a black hole Shelly, sucking people into you so you can expand while we have no choice but to collapse in on ourselves." They walked out and went to slam the door behind them but paused *to turn back one last time, "don't call me okay? We're nothing."*

"Sal."

"Nothing. Bye Shelly."

Kyra was walking back into the house when Sal stormed up the stairs. She snapped that she'd be in the car waiting and if Kyra wanted a way home she might want to think about saying a quick goodbye. Kyra set the snacks on the counter beside the pie and jogged down the stairs.

Shelly was still naked and wrapped in the blanket Sal had given her for her birthday in the tenth grade.

"What happened?"

Shelly just shook her head as tears and snot dripped from her face and she wiped it onto the blanket. Kyra pulled her into her chest and rubbed Shelly's back as she cried.

"I'm sorry I've gotta go, Sal's my ride and I don't really have any other way home. I'll come and visit you again soon okay?"

Shelly nodded against her shoulder and said a muffled "I love you."

"I love you too."

Kyra offered to help Shelly get dressed and back upstairs before she left but Shelly told her she wasn't worth helping and that she would just stay down there. Kyra tried to protest but Shelly had already rolled over and started crying into her pillow again, so Kyra closed the door and left.

▪

Shelly stayed in the bed until she had run out of tears and her blanket was more snot than fabric. She repeated the words to herself again, deni tsin nadint'i, qwaxezintan, she found comfort in the language, her language. And with it, she found the strength to pull herself out of the bed and get dressed. She knew there was no way she was going to make it up the stairs by herself. Her mother had been gone longer than she had expected and she didn't want to ask when she'd be home, it would only cause her to panic and that was something Shelly didn't need. From what Tom had said it seemed like Sam was confined to the bed for the next little while so she was out of the question. She decided to message Tom, they needed to talk anyways. She only had to wait about ten minutes before he showed up and helped her back upstairs.

They had become pretty close friends over the fishing trips and almost daily hangouts. He wasn't always there, but he was there enough.

Sam had explained to her that he wasn't her cousin by blood, that his dad had married her aunt Kiyana who was Marcus's sister, about three years ago. They had been friends before that and considered themselves cousins for the four years his dad and Kiyana had dated before they got married. But they said their bond was solidified in writing when the marriage certificate was signed. Shelly had laughed at her when she said it, like someone the marriage certificate of her aunt and his dad made them best friends for life in the eyes of the province. Sam had brushed her off and told her that was exactly what it did, then burst out laughing as well. When they had composed themselves Sam's demeanour changed and her tone turned serious. She said that one day his dad just disappeared. He'd gone out into the woods for his morning run like he always did and just never came back. The cops thought he had just run away, said they searched every inch of the forest and found nothing. That's why Sam and Tom and been out that day in the woods when they saw the creature. She told Shelly it really fucked Tom up for a while. He was sure that thing had his dad and wanted to try and find where it came from. He had talked about it for weeks and then one day he stopped. He never brought it up again and never went back into the woods near her house since that was where it all happened.

Shelly looked at him now, standing in the kitchen. He moved around the house so seamlessly, in a way she didn't even move around Kyra or Sal's house. She choked on the thought.

"Tom."

He looked up from the pie he had cut and was now wrapping up to put in the fridge.

"Was this your house?"

Tom froze, readjusted his shoulders, then put the pie in the fridge. He almost pulled off the nonchalant persona he was trying to portray aside from practically slamming the fridge.

He winced.

"Sorry," he said, "did Sam tell you?" He grew more eager, "have you talked to her?"

"No. I'm sorry I haven't. It's the way you move around the house. You don't really seem like a guest when you're here. Everything seems so natural and it makes sense why your dad-" She didn't catch herself fast enough.

He finished her thought, "why my dad was in these woods? Shelly, I want you to know I really wasn't trying to be rude when you came into the bar that first night. I know I already apologized but I wanted you to know why I said that. When Sam and I saw that thing we were looking for my dad."

"I know, she told me."

"Yeah I know she told me she did. But she didn't tell you that it was right around the same time her boyfriend had taken off with all her money and her best friend, right?"

Shelly shook her head.

"I didn't think so. We were out there, and we were both so.. empty. We were looking for something, for anything to fill that void. I still feel empty sometimes, less so now than I used to, but I still feel it. I think Sam feels less empty too. And that's why we haven't seen it again. But you had that same look that Sam used to get, the same look I saw in the mirror every day up until recently. I knew you guys had bought this house and Sam had mentioned that your mom said you had a dog so it seemed obvious you'd go into the forest. I didn't know if that's why we

saw it, but I've always had this feeling it was and I didn't want you to go out there and not come back when I could have at least tried to stop it from happening."

Shelly hugged her arms around Tom's waist and he rested his chin on the top of her head and hugged her back, basking in the feeling of friendship with someone outside of his cousin who couldn't even look at him.

That was when Cosmina walked back in and let out a loud "oop! Sorry, I didn't mean to interrupt."

Tom and Shelly quickly dropped their hug to avoid any unwanted and unwarranted comments and clarified that she hadn't interrupted anything. Shelly could tell she didn't believe them but she had other things to worry about at the moment.

They moved out of the kitchen for her mother to put the groceries away, told her Tom had brought a pie and it was in the fridge, then maybe a little too loudly, exclaimed that Edward needed to do his rehabilitation exercises and they would all be outside.

"So. Do you mind me asking where your friends went?"

Shelly rubbed her face in her hands and explained everything. She thought afterwards that she probably could have spared the whole orgasm part of it but figured that what she was going to tell him about her and Sam's trip to the woods would be far more scarring so she let it go without so much as an apology for the TMI.

"So you're into Sam, hey?"

"I must be if that's what came out of my mouth when I.. you know.." Her cheeks were hot all of a sudden, "but I think about Sal all the time. They're amazing, and so is Sam don't get me wrong. I'm just so confused with myself cause I didn't even know I really liked Sam that much. Sure, I had a little crush on her, she's hot and smart and hilarious. But whenever I'd think about her I'd start to feel really guilty and then I'd think of Sal and how great we would be together and I started to miss them so much I'd feel sick. I know what Sam's been through and

since I didn't know with Sal I didn't want to explore something with Sam and leave her hurt and alone."

"Well, now you know with Sal. I'd let things cool off with that a bit first, but I think you care enough about Sam that she's pretty safe with you."

"I thought I cared about Sal enough not to hurt them either and look how that went."

Tom put his hand on her shoulder, they had stopped walking at the edge of the driveway and were watching Edward walk slowly through the wildflowers that were now double what they had been when she had first moved. He didn't say anything, but his hand was comfort enough and Shelly knew he was telling her that it was okay and she had only made a mistake.

"Helping me up the stairs wasn't the only reason I asked you to come over."

"I thought as much"

She turned to him, the way Sam had turned to her when she told her about Tom's dad, "I need to tell you what we saw in the woods.

By the time Shelly had finished describing the sound they had heard, the coyotes, his severed body and crushed head, Tom looked like he was either going to pass out, throw up, or both.

"No wonder Sam didn't want to see me."

Shelly agreed and admitted that sometimes it was hard for her to look at him too but that she didn't want him to feel isolated and was trying her best to work through it. She waited a moment before starting up again and telling him about her dreams, the first one where the cowboy warned her, and the most recent one. She told him of the words he had spoken to her

deni tsin nadint'i. Tom tried to say them back but stumbled over the pronunciation. He asked her what they meant and she told him what the cowboy had translated for her. She told him about her grandmother and how she had sent the cowboy but she didn't know what to do now or how he was supposed to help her. Tom wished he knew but he didn't know anything about her culture or their practices or what any of it might mean.

"That's part of the problem. I don't really know much about my culture either. I know some of it of course. I would dipnet with my grandmother and grandfather when I would visit them, I would go with them to the powwows but I haven't learned any of the dances. My mom does make a lot of traditional food though that her mother taught her. Romani and Tsilhqot'in, which means Chilcotin."

"Romani? Like Romanian?"

"No, like Romani or Roma. Who the racists and xenophobes call gypsies."

"Oh! Cool, do you know anything about them at all?"

"Only a little. My great-grandmother, the one I'm named after, she was really proud of her culture and when she met her husband he had been fleeing a war on his people and he was scared so he assimilated as best he could. That's what my grandmother told me at least. So she practiced some of the traditions that her mother had taught her and passed those on to me and to my mom, but I think she always felt a little lost without that other half of her."

▪

After Tom had left Shelly and Edward made the difficult journey across the fifteen-foot stretch of the driveway to the front door. She was out of breath when she reached it and was thankful to see her father pulling up in the car he had been borrowing from Izac to go to and from different areas of the island that he liked to paint. He said this was the best move they had ever made, the scenery never got tired of being put to paper. He rushed out of the car and opened the door wide, curtsying as he did so. Shelly laughed at how ridiculous he looked with his paint-covered pants as he curtsied to her.

They walked into the house together, Shelly leaning on her father's arm for more stability than her crutches offered her.

Her mother was standing in the kitchen, staring at her phone. Her head snapped up when the three of them walked in.

"I need to tell you guys something."

Her mother looked stone-faced, and her father went over to her to rub her shoulders. She relaxed into him as she did so and her voice cracked when she spoke, "I like Tom, but he's at a different maturity level and I just think."

Shelly waved her arms in front of her and cut her off, "woah. No. Tom and I are nothing but friends. I wanted to tell you that I'm gay. I've known for quite a while now and I wanted to tell you."

"I don't understand." It was Aki who spoke.

Cosmina whirled on him, horrified, and Shelly's face fell, they both asked him what he meant by he didn't understand.

"Oh, no," he realized his mistake and tried to backpedal as tears started to well in both of their eyes, "I just don't understand why you didn't tell us sooner."

Shelly asked if they could take the conversation to the living room and talk there. She and her father sat on the couch and Cosmina paced the length of the room, drumming her fingers on her legs as she did so. Shelly explained that she didn't know why but she had been scared that they might reject her even though it went against their nature to do so. When they asked her if she was a lesbian she told them she didn't know, that she didn't like boys and she knew that for sure but that she had liked Sal who didn't identify with any gender so she was still figuring out exactly what the label was.

It was at that point that her mother finally broke and tears began to flow from her eyes in large, heavy droplets. she collapsed into her husband's lap and reached for Shelly's hand, squeezing it tightly.

"I'm so sorry Shelly this has nothing to do with what you just told us," her voice was muffled against Aki's legs.

He rubbed her back and tried to get her to sit up and explain what was going on. It took her several tries. Each time she looked at Shelly the tears started up again.

Finally, following her daughter's method from early in the day, she cried out all her tears and was able to form a few half-coherent sentences, "I got a call... when you were outside with Tom. My... my mom..." she choked on the words, "she's gone. They took her. And she's gone." She fell back into her husband's lap as he tried to ask her what she meant by they took her, but Shelly knew.

She could already feel the corners of their house darkening, the breeze shifting and bringing something evil with it. Coyotes howled and yipped in the far distance and when Cosmina finally sat up again and looked at her daughter who now shook with fear and anger and loss, she screamed.

Part Two

Chapter 1

beginnings

Cecilia

It was the same as it was every night. Cecilia nestled herself into bed, pulled her blankets down to her hips so she didn't get wrapped up in them and closed her eyes. Sleep came quickly, it dug its claws in and snuffed out all the lights, making escape nearly impossible. It was a kind of capture that she had gotten used to in the past year, once the dreams had started. They were almost always the same with only slight variations here and there. In the fall, through to the spring, the dream often contained rain as her subconscious heard the drumming of it off the tin roof above her head. She often thought of it as her ancestors reaching out to her, letting her know through their songs that they were there and that they would keep her safe in the journey ahead.

▪

She thought of her ancestors often, though hardly spoke of them to save her mother the pain. She had been removed from her family young and taken to a school run by the church. Her braids had been removed and her hair cut, severing her from her ancestors, her traditions and her homeland. She had spent ten years at the school and her hair had not been allowed to grow one inch passed where it had been cut. She watched as her friends, her cousins, her brothers and sisters were brought to the school and taken in the night. On the mornings that would follow these nights, the priests and the nuns would come out into the dining hall blowing a piercing whistle that drew everyone's attention to them. They would give a speech about how the taken child had misbehaved, how they had attacked a school official, braided their hair, found an eagles feather and kept it beneath their pillow, and how these actions had consequences, how they would be sent to a new school, one for bad kids who misbehaved. Of course, they all knew there was no other school, no place for bad kids. They lived in terror, in an inescapable jail manned by the power of God. It was on the day she graduated, alongside only a hand full of the children, now nearly adults, who had joined her in her first year, that she met Cecilia's father. He once was a businessman, now a soldier, on his return from the war. He had seen her mother step off the bus and was instantly struck by her beauty, her chopped dark hair, her almond eyes of the darkest brown, and the slender frame that had so clearly been underfed. He was thirteen years her senior with a young son and no living wife. He had offered her a life of security, so she accepted. She was not a naive woman, and she knew how the world saw her, how little she would have had she not taken him at his word. He was not a bad man, he cared for her, and tended to her, he held her when she cried on their wedding day when she learned that their marriage had stripped her of her identity. And she cared for him, she was thankful for him in the help he had offered, for the land and the money he had left her when the cancer began to spread, and she love him for the daughter they had brought into this world together.

-

It was this story her mother had told her when she could no longer take Cecilia's questions that had made her finally stop asking. She had seen how her mother still kept her hair cut neatly at her shoulders, making sure to only cut it with rusted kitchen scissors as a reminder of those who had been taken in the night. She saw the way her mother's heart would weep when she would walk amongst the wheat fields and fall to her knees when the rain would come and the first night of drumming would begin. She heard the songs her mother sang when she thought Cecilia couldn't hear. Songs that came from deep within her and danced from her throat. They were songs from a lost world sung in a language Cecilia did not understand, but still, she listened and she learned. At first, she followed the tunes, humming them to herself as she went about her chores. Then she learned the words, and with them, she learned meaning, not through translation but through feeling. She did not know what her mother sang, only that some nights she sang of family, others she sang in prayer to her Creator, and others she sang in sorrow and mourning. Then she learned how to make the words and the tunes dance from her throat the way her mother had. At first, they had come out harsh and guttural as if somehow the words and the rhythms she had longed to understand were mocking her. She tried for months to sing with beauty. Stepping out into the forest to practice with the woods watching eyes. It wasn't until the rain came again that she was able to imitate her mother's voice. She had been in the woods when she heard the first beat, a soft plop as a raindrop hit the yellow leaves of the poplars above her. Then all at once the cloud released itself onto her. The rain beat against the trees, against the grasses, against her skin. It was then that she began to sing, and the words had seemed to wrap around her feet, dancing in unison with her. She dug in her toes and spread her arms wide, stepping and turning, dipping one arm, then the other. She closed her eyes and saw women dressed in bright beaded dresses adorned in feathers, their hair braided in long black rows down their backs. Eagle feathers pointed to the sky from the back of their heads as they matched each of Cecilia's steps, her joy, her words. The woods were filled with the sounds of native voices, Chilcotin voices, and then suddenly they were gone. The rain had stopped and the forest had quieted. Cecilia had opened her eyes and made her way home, content not to tell her mother what she had seen. But when she had walked through the door and dripped water into the kitchen, her mother's eyes had filled with tears, and Cecilia could see that she somehow knew.

It was that night that the dreams had started. There had been no rain that night, and no rain for countless nights after that. Cecilia had closed her eyes, tucked neatly into a pile of blankets pulled all the way to her chin and drifted off to sleep. She dreamt of an old man, his eyes were sunken so deeply behind a dropping brow she couldn't even make out the colour. The muscles had all but detached themselves from his cheekbones and now hung lazily in a mass of white skin. He wore a beaver pelt over his left shoulder and had a red feathered arrow sticking out the other. When he walked his feet barely left the ground making a shuck shuck noise as they drug in the sand beneath him. Cecilia tried to step back but couldn't. Each step she took only propelled her forwards, towards his outstretched hands. She squeezed her eyes shut as his frail bones gripped her shoulder with the strength of a younger man. She stood there a long while, unwavering in the stench that made its way from the man's mouth to her nose on a breath that shook from his lungs into the depth of her. Finally, he loosened the grip of his right hand. He drew his thumb along her forehead, from the prominent widow's peak to the crease of her brow, then across its middle from left to right. She shuttered at the feeling of the cross, a symbol as unholy as its bearers deemed it otherwise and forced her eyes open. The man in front of her no longer wore a beaver pelt, and the arrow had been replaced with a decorative cloth draped over the shoulders of a no longer frail man in a yellowed white robe. On his head sat a mitre below which were empty holes where his eyes should be.

When he removed his hand from her he simply stood in front of her. Waiting. She wanted to move but even though his hand was gone his grip was not and it was clasped so tightly around her shoulders, her chest, and her throat that she suddenly thought the air would stop coming and that this would be the last thing she saw before she died.

In the distance, far past the eyeless priest, in the darkest parts of the desert that she was unable to touch, she heard the howl of a pack of coyotes. They called to her and the harsh sounds of their voices made her itch for the waking world, for any world aside from this.

There was a movement, the priest. He was reaching for her again, for eyes. He needed them a voice had whispered to her as he reached toward her face. She couldn't let him have them. She clenched her eyes shut and told herself to wake up, wake up, just wake up!

She thrashed wildly in her bed, the blankets wrapped tightly around her, cut off her air supply. She told herself to calm down, that she was in her bed, that she could unwrap herself from the blankets and she would be fine.

▪

She was fourteen when the dreams started. Her brother had just turned twenty and brought his new wife to the farm. She was a Catholic and insisted on bowing her head to pray before each meal. Her mother had hated every minute of it but in the eyes of the law her brother was the owner of the land and the leader of the household, and most importantly, he did not care for her mother's wishes in the slightest.

He had hated her from the start and hated Cecilia even more. Her mother always said she didn't know where it came from, his father had been a kind and compassionate man and he had turned into the devil himself. Of course, she knew where it had come from. His mother's family had been religious and of the opinion that the best thing that had ever happened to the native people of the land they now occupied, was their education in religion taught by the Catholic Church. Sometimes Cecilia wondered to herself if her father had known about the cancer all along, and that he married her mother to repent for the evil he had stood behind for so long. He died when she was nine, making her brother the head of the household and the family accounts at only fifteen. His father, of course, had left the land to her mother, in legal terms she did own it. But the lawyers and the bankers and the judges told her she had two options; stay on the farm, let the son run the accounts and the land and the title remained in her name, or fight it in court and lose everything. She took the latter option and remained on the farm since she had nowhere else to go. That suited her brother fine, he was now a man of luxury, or so he liked to present as. He blew through the money within the year and her mother didn't do a thing to stop him. She knew how to farm and he didn't so he took off to the city to find work and Cecilia and her mother stayed and worked the land. She felt a connection to her ancestors, and to her mother when they cut the wheat and husked the corn when they milked and fed the cows and plucked the eggs from the chicken coop.

They lived like this for four years and Cecilia thought those had been the only four years her mother had truly been happy. Those were the years when she sang in the fields and hummed the tunes while she cooked. Then one day, her brother returned with a blonde-haired girl on his arm. She couldn't remember much about her aside from the blonde hair, and the fact she had a knack for being nasty with a smile on her face.

▪

They lived with them for another six years. Cecilia had been homeschooled and when she went to the high school to take the final exams in the year she turned 18, she passed with the highest grades ever recorded for their district. The board fought it and she settled with not having her test scores released and only receiving one paper copy of her grades to take to universities. Not that it mattered, the principal had said, no one wants a thing like you there anyways. He had poked her in the chest when he said it and Cecilia had looked him dead in the face and told him he was the most pathetic excuse for a man she'd ever seen. She said it with a toothy grin and cheerful wave as she turned and walked away. Her brother's wife had been good for one thing. Teaching her how to be a cold-hearted bitch when she needed to be.

On her walk home that evening she had snatched an onion from the market and peeled it before the last turn in the driveway where the house came into view. She put it as close to her eye as she could and waited until the tears started to trickle down her cheeks which she then pinched to redden. She tossed the onion into the field and made her way into the house, feigning defeat and failure. Her brother told her he always knew she couldn't do it and his wife remarked on how awful it was that she would be stuck here with them forever. She had gotten more hateful after the second kid popped out. Cecilia felt sorry for the girls, their dad was a deadbeat who married about his class to suck all the money out from his inlaws, and their mom was a good-for-nothing racist bitch who hid her disdain for others behind the virtue of God. Cecilia didn't really blame her for that part though, it was what all good Catholics and Christians did.

▪

It was two more years before she left. Two years, three months, and twelve days to be exact. That was how many days her mother had been sick. It started the day she came home from the exams. It might have started before but it was only noticeable then. She didn't know what it was and didn't want any doctors around her so she lived with it.

It was a terrible thing and Cecilia could hardly look at her by the end of it all. It sucked the life from her. Pulled the skin taught against her bones, drained her of colour until her skin, hair, and even her eyes had turned grey. Her teeth had all fallen out and black spots grew in patches all across her body. About a year in Cecilia finally broke down and called a doctor. They told her they had never seen anything like it and would be of no use to her nor did they want to be. It was a year after this her mother asked her to come in closer so she could speak. She could hardly move her arm she was so weak but she managed to beckon for Cecilia to come down close to her mouth. Her breath was rancid and Cecilia had to cover her nose to keep from gagging.

Her mother's voice shook and sounded like it was being pushed through a bagpipe, "I know you passed," she took a deep breath, "your exams."

Cecilia sat back up and looked at her mother with surprise. She hadn't told anyone that, not even her. She had been too worried that the sickness might mess with her mind, that it might make her forget who she could and couldn't trust and she would let it slip to her brother or worse his wife.

"How did you know that?"

Her mother moved her mouth, trying to speak. Her lips moved up and down like a fish taken from the water as it gasps in the air. Cecilia bent back down.

"Under," another breath, "the floor." And with that, she reached out a shaky finger and pointed to a piece in the floor that had once had a knot in the wood that was now an empty hole. Cecilia got up and opened the door the check the hall. It was empty. She closed it again and made her way to the hole in the floor.

She bent down slowly, making as little sound as possible in case someone was in the room below her and wondered what all of her "sneaking around" had been about, as they would put it. She had learned very quickly that a person couldn't do anything in that house without someone watching or listening to their every move. She quietly popped the floorboard out of its place and reached her hand down into the dust and rat-shit-covered boards beneath it. She didn't feel anything at first and bent further down, searching along the length of the boards now. Then she felt it, a long wooden box. She slowly pulled it out, careful not to hit it off of anything and alert their unwanted guests. When she finally had it out from the floor she saw it had a raven carved into it in the traditional style of her people. Pulling it open she had to bite her tongue to stifle the gasp that nearly left her mouth. Inside was a stack of bills that added up to five hundred dollars, and a golden locket with a picture of a young boy in it.

She held it to her chest and then hurriedly put it back into its box and its place in the floorboards as she heard the creak of the stairs. The bed squeaked as she sat back down beside her mother and held her hand, thanking her.

"Cecilia, you've been in here an awfully long time. What have you been up to," her brother's wife inspected the room and scrunched her nose as she always did on the next line, "sneaking around? Doing something you shouldn't?"

Cecilia smiled at her sweetly, "this is what happens when you're actually lovable, your parents what you beside them in their final moments."

Her brother's wife just smiled and told her dinner had gotten cold while she was up there so she'd just go ahead and throw it away since she was sure Cecilia wouldn't want cold food.

-

Three months and twelve days after that her mother took her last breath and Cecilia was glad to see her suffering end.

Her brother's family had been at church when it happened and Cecilia wasted no time. She packed her clothes, and the few books she had, grabbed the box from under the floorboards and wrote her brother a letter. In it, she wrote that she had called the coroner and he would be out in the evening to remove her mother's body and give her a proper burial and that she was taking the second car as it was legally in her mother's name. She also let him know that she had a copy of her mother's will and had already taken a second copy to the courthouse and she was willing to let him live on the farm until he died but that the property would be staying in her name, and if he wished to contest it she would make sure his pretty little money doll knew about the affair he'd been having since they had their first child.

She placed the note against the jar of milk she had taken out of the fridge and placed it on the table to bask in the heat of the day.

Then she walked out of the door which she left wide open, got into her mother's car, and drove down the driveway one last time.

Chapter 2

an affair

She had been in Vancouver for two years now. In the mornings she would wake up, go to the market down the street from her small apartment and buy an apple, a pint of milk, and a muffin. Then she would walk along the waters of English Bay and eat her breakfast while she watched the sunrise. This, of course, was only the routine she followed on days that rain didn't flood the streets and chill her to the bone on her short commute to and from the office. On those days, the rainy ones, she would walk to the market and then return home to watch the water droplets chase each other down her window pane to see who would make it to the sill first. She always cheered for the one that started off in last place and would trace it with her finger as it moved sporadically along the other side of the glass. She did this to avoid watching the women in their warehouse and factory uniforms walk past her home as they swung their steel lunch boxes and chatted amongst themselves. It wasn't that she didn't think women should be working such jobs or casually wearing dirt coveralls. If anything she hoped that the men returning from war would have more appreciation for what the women had contributed during their time away, that maybe when they got back they would make changes that gave the women more sovereignty over their lives. She knew it was a pipe dream but there was some hope to be had she would think as she watched her water droplet. No, her problem with the women was their effortless chatter and the bursts of laughter that often accompanied it. It made her lonely and somehow made her apartment feel even more empty and smaller than it already was. Two years and she still hadn't made any real friends aside from one, Seline.

She had a few ladies she would speak to occasionally; Edith, the one who ran the market, Helen, the one who worked at the laundromat, and Seline, her boss's wife. Seline had actually gotten her the job and helped her to get into university when she had first arrived and pleaded with the admissions officer to let her apply to the school and been turned away. Seline had watched the whole thing from a chair in the corner of the office where visitors sat in wait for university officials to make time to see them. She had gotten up and grabbed Cecilia's elbow to stop her from leaving and asked her to wait a moment. Then she asked the admissions officer to borrow the phone, dialled a number and spoke in a hushed voice to someone on the other end before handing the receiver to the officer. Cecilia hadn't heard what she said and at the time didn't know who she had called, although she now knew it had been her husband who was a recent graduate from the top of his class and a newly successful lawyer. The officer's face changed from smug to shocked to guilty in a matter of seconds.

-

"Hey," he had grumbled at Cecilia as he held out his hand for her transcript.

When she stood to give it to him she had looked at the woman in disbelief. No one had shown her kindness like that before and she wasn't quite sure what to make of it. She went to speak but before she could get the words out the woman held up a hand and told her not to worry about it.

"I'm Seline," she extended her hand to Cecilia.

"Cecilia," she shook it.

"If you don't mind me asking, what are you hoping to study here?"

"I was hoping to study politics, then get my law degree."

Seline looked at her with surprise and admiration. She studied Cecilia a moment before reaching into her purse. Her head was still tilting down as she spoke and rummaged through her back, slightly muffling her words.

"That's incredibly ambitious. I hope you don't mind I peeked over your shoulder and was quite impressed with your transcript," she pulled something out of her purse, a business card, which she handed to Cecilia, "my husband just opened a law firm, if you're interested in a job you should stop by."

With that Seline had left and Cecilia stood standing in the office of the university, staring at the card. She had thought to herself that it couldn't be real, she was finally going to leave her crappy job chopping up fish heads at the market and work in a real law firm. There wasn't a single moment of doubt or hesitation and it was that same day she had walked into her old job at quit.

▪

Now in her third semester at university Cecilia was already classified as a full semester ahead. She had taken extra summer courses and an extra course through both semesters that she completed during night classes. In her spare time, she worked as a part-time assistant for John, Seline's husband. He was an intense individual who seldom smiled and often spoke to Cecilia in a military sort of way, but he was never cruel. Cecilia had admired that he was able to be so firm yet hold so much empathy in him. She always thought it must have been because of Seline. To be married to a Japanese Canadian woman, especially during the time of the war could not have been easy. He had spent his time with his new firm advocating for the removal of Japanese concentration camps in Canada and he and Cecilia often spent time looking into ways to help those who had been detained.

It was during one of their weekend sessions of sorting through newspaper clippings in search of names for those they could help, jotting down their last known addresses, typing out their stories, and figuring out if there was any legal action that could be taken in their favour when she had met Andrei.

▪

The door to the room opened hesitantly and a broad-shouldered man whose head Cecilia thought might hit the ceiling when he extended to full height, stuck his head through the frame.

"Is this John Chamber's office?"

John had gone to get them more coffee and a couple of scones from his apartment above their offices. He always said he didn't want to disturb Seline and the children by asking her to bring them down, so he often times went up.

Cecilia stood from her newspaper clippings and smoothed out her dress before walking over to the door that the man had now opened. He wasn't as tall as Cecilia had originally thought, but he was still taller than most at around 6'3".

"This is. Can I help you?"

The man removed his hat and held it to his chest with a bow of his head before extending his hand out to her, "I'm Andrei, the new partner. Pleasure."

Before Cecilia could speak and tell him she had no idea who he was or that a new partner was even starting, John walked into the room from the back door that led out to the fire escape. He always used the fire escape for some reason that Cecilia was yet to figure out.

"Andrei!" John set the cups of coffee and scones down on the table and happily jaunted over to the man now known as Andrei and clasped his hand with a firm shake, "I see you've met Cecilia."

"I have. She's very pleasant," his eyes lit up at her and she blushed at the big toothy grin he flashed her way.

She turned to John, "you never mentioned a new partner."

"My lord. You're right. I apologize. But now we are all on the same page and can continue with our work. Andrei, tell me, you're here early, why?"

"I'd rather not share the circumstances under which I've come to arrive before my expected time."

Cecilia stared at him. No one had over-spoken to John that way before, no one aside from her. Even though he had spoken with a soft tone he had directly denied an answer to John's question. This seemed to shock John as well, however, he quickly recovered. He had spoken with an odd accent Cecilia had thought, some kind of Eastern European maybe? She wasn't sure and felt invasive asking.

"Very well, your life is your own. Do you have a place to stay?"

"I was hoping to stay at my new apartment but when I arrived I was turned away on account of arriving earlier than expected," they had moved toward the table now and he reached for one of the cups of coffee.

John stopped him, "that is actually Cecilia's. If you would like a cup I can go and make another."

Andrei turned to Cecilia looking embarrassed, "my apologies," then he turned back to John, "if it's not too much trouble I would enjoy a coffee myself."

John nodded his head and made his way back to the fire escape.

Cecilia sat down at the table and took a sip from her cup before biting into a scone and offering to halve it with Andrei. He politely declined the offer and looked around at the offices, letting out a whistle.

He looked at Cecilia, "how long have you worked here?"

"Almost two years. I'm only here part-time though, I'm studying politics at the university here."

Andrei raised his eyebrows, "impressive. John is lucky to work with such a smart woman, and by the look of things, a strong one."

Cecilia wasn't sure if he was talking about her physique or the aura of the room. He may have been referring to the fact she sat side by side with her boss and worked on the same projects he did. She found out later he had meant all of it.

She had just opened her mouth to speak when John burst back into the room, Seline in tow. She gave Cecilia a strange look and moved her eyes between her and Andrei before settling her eyes on him.

"Seline," she extended her hand and he shook it.

"Andrei, it's a pleasure to meet you."

John clasped his wife's shoulder and handed Andrei his cup, "Seline has had a wonderful idea. Cecilia has a couch you can sleep on until your apartment is completed," Cecilia moved to protest but John held up a hand to stop her before she could, "now I know it is unconventional for a man to stay with an unmarried woman, especially if there is no intention to marry, or any acquaintance between the two, but it will only be for a month.

Cecilia choked, "a month!"

Andrei stood up and looked at Cecilia who was still sitting, "no. That won't be necessary. I can find a hotel."

"Nonsense. You can stay with Cecilia."

She levelled her eyes at John who tilted his head toward his wife who in turn gave Cecilia another funny look, "fine."

Seline clapped, "great! Shelly, why don't you come have your coffee with me while John fills Andrei in on your project, I'd like to speak with you a moment."

"Seline, dear, please refrain from using friendly names in the office."

Seline rolled her eyes, "all right. Cecilia would you please join me upstairs for coffee."

"Of course," she grabbed her cup and followed Seline out of the main doors and up the stairs to their apartments.

-

"Sorry dear," Seline said as she opened the door for them, "John wanted you down there with them but I wanted to speak with you privately."

They made their way into the living room and turned on the radio so the children wouldn't hear them. A soft jazz tune played and filled the air with a lighter mood than had previously been there. Cecilia loved her friend but sometimes Seline interjected herself in places she shouldn't and often times pulled her away from work she wanted to be involved in simply because she wanted to chat. She was also annoyed at her for suggesting Andrei stay with her. Odd things happened at her apartment and she preferred to keep those things to herself. She didn't need Andrei telling people that there were things that went bump in the night and odd shadows that flung themselves across the walls when no light was there to create them.

They sat opposite each other. Seline was spread out on the couch, and Cecilia sat in the armchair by the window that was usually reserved for John.

"I wanted to speak to you about Andrei."

"Well, I would have appreciated it if we could have had this discussion before you invited him to stay with me."

"I know. I'm sorry, but he's been through an awful lot and I thought that it might be nice for him to be around someone who might understand him. Now before you ask, it's not my place to say what it is that I know but I am certain he will tell you. Plus, you're such a beautiful girl and I know you're not interested in finding a husband at the moment, but he is a very handsome, very smart, very kind man. And I didn't see any harm in trying to bring you two together."

"Of course, you don't see any harm, you're already married and being married is your whole life. I want more than that. I'm not some housewife who wants to cook and clean and clean up after children all day, I want to actually be someone."

She regretted the words before they left her mouth and her eyes dropped in shame when she saw the look of hurt on her friend's face. Seline wrung her dress in her hands and took a shaky breath.

"I wanted to be someone too you know."

Cecilia spoke quietly, shame still filled her and made its way into her vocal cords, "I know. That wasn't fair of me. I'm sorry. You're an amazing mother and a wonderful friend and I'm sorry you weren't able to follow your dreams."

Seline stopped wringing her dress and told Cecilia she forgave her but would like her to remember that she wasn't the only one who wanted something that seemed impossible to get, "some of us only have the luxury of giving up," she said.

Cecilia looked up at her now and moved to the couch to pull her friend whose eyes were now filled with tears, into her arms. They sat like this for a long time before Cecilia spoke again.

"I haven't lived with anyone other than my family, and John is one of the only men I've met who treats me like a person, who doesn't make me feel like I'm not safe in my own skin. I don't know this man and I'm not sure what skin he prefers for me yet."

"I know that, but John would never have hired him if he thought he was like the rest of them," she held both of Cecilia's hands in hers, "I promise you."

▪

Cecilia made her way back into the office, Seline had stayed behind in the apartment after reassuring her again that Andrei was going to be a fine roommate for the month he was with her.

"It really is okay," Andrei was saying to John, "I do not want to inconvenience Cecilia. A hotel will do just fine for me."

"It's fine."

Andrei jumped at Cecilia's words. He turned to face her and again stated a hotel would be fine for him. Cecilia waved his concerns off and assured him it was all right and she had just been caught off guard.

-

They walked down the street together. Passing war posters promoting enlistment, promoting women applying to factories, promoting war bonds, promoting really anything that might help out the war effort. Andrei seemed to shrink away from them as they passed by and when they crossed the street Cecilia made sure to position herself between him and the posters.

"So, where are you from."

No answer.

"Okay, none of my business. How long have you been in Canada?"

No reply again.

"Look, I don't mean to be rude, but if you're going to be staying with me I need to know something about you. How old are you?"

"I'm 27."

She nodded at this and couldn't think of anything else to say, so they walked in silence. She hadn't noticed it before but he walked with a bit of a slouch, not much, but enough that if you were paying attention you could see he wasn't as sure of himself as he first appeared. His eyes, though friendly had a sad look to them, a loneliness she thought, and there were dark circles that she also hadn't seen in the office. When he swallowed he did so sharply and the Adam's apple in his throat seemed to bob back up quicker than most of the men she had met.

"This is us," she stopped in front of her building and pulled out a collection of keys on a silver loop.

The long silver key with the square end opened the door to the building, she sifted through the collection and found it quickly. She turned it in the lock and pushed open the door with her shoulder as she turned the knob. The door was quite heavy and she had found that leverage always seemed to help. Andrei reached above her with his free hand and held the door for her to lead the way up the stairs.

Her apartment was on the fourth floor, second door to the right of the stairs. It had a large brass number 16 on it and was painted bright blue. She wasn't sure why but the owner had decided to paint the doors of each floor a ridiculously bright colour. The fourth floor was blue, the third was yellow, the second was green, and the first was red. She had noticed Andrei looking inquisitively at the doors whenever she rounded one of the corners to head to the next flight of stairs and wondered if he might be able to figure out the mystery. The door to the apartment was as heavy as the door to the building and when she inserted the large gold key with the diamond end and turned, she used her shoulder to push it open as well. She appreciated that Andrei held the door for her to lead the way but never felt the need to push the door open. He didn't think her incapable and it made her feel a little less uneasy about him being in her home.

"Welcome," she gestured to the apartment.

It was a simple one-bedroom. There was a tattered couch that one of Seline's friends had been giving away and so gave to Cecilia when she had first started at the firm, a small side table with a radio, and a small tea table with two chairs to match that was pushed against the kitchen window. Every surface of the apartment had been covered in plants and some even hang from the ceiling, she found it made her feel more at home and less like she was staying in an empty box like the stray cat she had found on the street that now lay lazily on the back of the tattered couch. Andrei walked over and stroked the cat's head, "what's his name?"

"Cat."

"Cat?"

"I found him on the street last year, he seemed old enough to already have a name and I didn't want to be rude by giving him another, so his name's cat."

Andrei pondered this a moment before holding up his suitcase and asking where he should put it.

"You can put it in the bedroom, I'll stay on the couch," she didn't let Andrei object, "you're a guest. The bed can be yours."

"Thank you."

Andrei followed the one narrow hallway to the bedroom at the end of it. On the right of the hallway was a small bathroom with a claw foot tub and across from that was a small storage closet. The bedroom like the rest of the house had plenty of plants in it and not much else. A twin-size bed sat on a spring-loaded metal bed frame, at the end of which sat a dresser with nothing on it but the wooden box Cecilia's mom had given her, and a photo of her and her mother when she was a young girl that had been propped up against the box. Beside the bed was the matching side table to the one beside the couch and on it sat a neatly arranged stack of watercolour papers on top of a sketchbook, with small tubes of paint lined up in a perfect according to colour, two paint brushes that had been perfectly cleaned, and a tin pencil container.

He placed his suitcase on the bed and waited a moment, wondering if Cecilia was going to leave him be or if she planned on watching him go through his bag. She stood there, understanding what he was waiting for and not caring, this was her house and she had a right to know what kind of man was staying with her. She assumed he understood this when he pressed the brass tabs and popped open the suitcase.

She moved toward him, peering into the small world Andrei had brought into her home. A black waistcoat with large silver buttons, black pants, a notebook, and nothing else.She gave Andrei a puzzled look.

"That's all you have?"

He sat on the bed and let his broad shoulders slump, "I didn't have much time to pack."

His accent was heavy and Cecilia liked the way it reverberated through her.

"I didn't either, when I left home," she wandered to the bed and sat on the opposite side of the suitcase, she gestured to the apartment, "most of this was here when I moved in. That or Seline gave it to me."

"She seems nice."

"She is."

"Can I tell you something?"

"I suppose I can't say no. You are staying in my house, whether or not I want to hear it you can say it and I have to listen."

"You're very odd."

"That's what you wanted to tell me?"

"No," he picked at his nails, a habit she found familiar in her own anxieties, "I am not here as the man most people think I am. John knows, but no one else, and it is such a heavy burden to carry the weight of pretending to be someone you are not."

Cecilia nodded. She could understand this and thought that he must realize that if he thought it was safe to open up to her about it.

"I am from Romania, as people think, I was born there. But I am Romani."

"Romani? I'm sorry, I'm not familiar with the term."

"Travellers. We are people who do not live the way standard society wants us to, and for that we are persecuted. My people, my family, have been hunted and driven away for as long as we have existed. And now... with the Nazi regime, it's much worse. That is why I am here earlier than expected. John helped me to flea, to hide from the German army and he had secured passage for my parents and my sister," he looked down now, trying to hide the redness that had reached his

eyes, "but they found us and they took them. I got away and I thought that Andreea, my sister, had as well."

At the mention of his sister he stopped trying to hide the tears altogether and they started to fall in heavy bursts, forcing his breath to catch and his shoulders to heave with each inhalation. Cecilia felt her own tears coming and reached a hand to his shoulder for comfort.

▪

After the first night Cecilia and Andrei found comfort in the fact that they no longer had to feel as if they were alone in the world with no one to understand them. And when Andrei moved out to his own apartment the following month, Cecilia was devastated to see him go. They still spent time together in the office, more time in Seline's opinion than people who were just co-workers. She always said this with a playful jab at Cecilia's side that often times made her blush. She guessed that was why, four years later when they announced they were going on their first official outing as a couple, neither John nor Seline seemed overly excited or surprised. Not that they weren't happy for them, Seline began planning the wedding the very next day when Cecilia finally felt willing to tell her about her true feelings for Andrei and John gave her a raise the moment Seline mentioned the possibility of marriage to him.

▪

Within two months they were married and John and Seline had been their only witnesses. They were happy to have it that way and even happier when John decided to throw them a party in commemoration of starting their own firm in the year following the completion of Cecilia's law degree. She had been worried that he would be mad, or feel betrayed by them. He had felt that once before, when he had caught them together in the office after hours. Andrei's pants had been pulled down to his ankles and he was bending over her, her back on a table with the top of her dress pulled down to her waist and her legs *up on his shoulders. John thought that someone had broken in and had rushed downstairs to see what the commotion was about only to find two of his employees, unwed, and in the middle of very passionate sex. He told them it wasn't entirely the sex outside of matrimony that bothered him, though that was part of it, but the fact they were using his office as a place to commit such acts. Cecilia had been so ashamed that she stopped having sex with Andrei all together until they were married. Which, if they were being truthful, was part of the reason they had rushed into the wedding.*

▪

Following their departure from the firm they moved into a small house on the other side of the city. They still visited John and Seline once a week and often times spent the night on their couch after drinking too much wine. The two of them were happy, and for the first five years the dreams had stopped all together and the corners of their bedroom weren't as dark as before.

Chapter 3

the bad side of things

She wretched, her stomach heaving spastically. Trying desperately to push up something anything, but there was nothing left. She had emptied the contents of her stomach hours ago, but still, she heaved over the tin bucket between her feet on the marble floor. The room around her had a fresh coat of paint on the walls, blue with a greyish tint to it. Andreea had chosen the colour for the room, her room, one she would soon share with her baby brother. There was a window on the left wall of the room and Cecilia had pulled the curtain wide to flood the room with sunlight despite her head's aversion to the light lately.

Sweat beaded and crowded onto her brow. Another fit of retching and more bile. This time the flips and twists of her stomach had been too much and Cecilia fell to her knees on the floor to leave behind the soft cushion of Andreea's bed.

She had begun to shiver as she felt an intense chill entering the room.

"Andrei," Cecilia called desperately between fits of bile and spit falling from her lips, "Andrei they're back! They're back!"

Tears fell into the bucket, making small ripples in the yellow liquid that sloshed at its bottom. Cecilia kept her eyes fixed on the bucket below. She didn't dare look up. She didn't need to. She knew what was awaiting her eyes across the room and had seen it enough times, felt it enough times to know it was there.

"Mommy?"

"Not now baby, get daddy, tell daddy mommy needs him okay?

"Are you okay?"

"Get your father Andreea!"

Cecilia hated to yell at her and tried her best to always be calm and understanding with her daughter. But not when the chills began, when the chills began she couldn't help it. It was as though darkness was consuming her and pushing her towards anger and fear. She didn't need to see Andreea's face to know that she had hurt her. She knew all too well the hanging head of disappointment that came along with disappointing one's parents. She knew the feeling of hot cheeks and sore eyes from trying to stop the tears when voices were raised and you didn't understand why. She sighed, then wretched again.

"My love, please. Let me take you to the hospital, this is killing you." Andrei had always loved his wife more than anything in the world, and an unborn child was not something he was willing to lose her over.

He bent now and placed his arm on her back. He moved it in small, slow circles as another round of bile hit the bucket. She was still beautiful even when she had her face crammed into a bucket of toxic waste. He bent his head to her shoulder and let out a sigh as his forehead stuck to her skin from the sweat that engulfed her body.

"There's nothing here my love."

Cecilia took a rattled breath as more tears streamed toward the bucket. Her voice cracked as she let out a faint whisper, as though pleading with her husband, "they're there."

Andrei's own eyes now began to well and he could feel the heat rising in his cheeks as he looked once more around the room. He took his time, staring at every corner of the room, every small bit of darkness to see if he could see what his wife saw. No matter how hard he strained, there was nothing that looked even remotely similar to what his wife had described to him. No tall man made of darkness, no looming figures, no jagged-edged shadows, but there was a staleness in the air. This he attributed to his wife's health.

"It's the house Andrei, this damn house, you have to listen to me."

"It's not the house my love."

"It's. This. Damn. House," she practically cawed the words at him, screeching the words out like some feral bird.

He pulled her into him and she let her weight fall into his chest.

"I'm sorry," was all she said.

▪

They had managed to find the only doctor in the city willing to perform the procedure and it cost them nearly all of their savings. Andrei said he hadn't minded much and that they had enough clients that the money would be back in no time. He held her hand through it all, forcing himself to keep his eyes open. If she had to experience the removal of her child in its sixth month with nothing to take away the pain and nothing to ease the terror, then he would do what he could to make sure she didn't have to go through it alone. Andreea had been left at home with Seline to watch over her and all Cecilia could think of was not making it back to her. She had cried to Andrei about it in the car and he had had to force her into the doctors office. Of course she knew this was the only way, that this pregnancy would kill her if she saw it through, but there was still the possibility that trying to save her would kill her anyways.

Andrei saw her eyes flick to the corner of the room and he knew what she could see there.

"Hey," he spoke softly, "look at me. Okay? Look at me my love."

She tore her eyes away from the darkness and looked at her husband. She loved him and how safe one glimpse into his eyes made her feel. She held his gaze, trying to stay in that feeling of safety forever. Then her vision began to blur and the air started to feel heavy in her chest. She could hear the muffled sound of Andrei calling her name. The last thing she saw before she fainted was a faceless yet somehow grinning shadow standing over her husbands shoulder.

Chapter 5

the shadows

Andreea

Her mother had always told her that the room at the top of the staircase was off-limits. Of course, she was still allowed upstairs, just not in the room that was directly in front of the staircase, the room with the purple door. Too many toxic chemicals and paints that might make her sick was always the excuse. A pretty bad excuse considering she was fourteen and knew better than to stick her hand in a vat of oil paint cleaner and see what it tasted like, but she never argued. Her mother might have been a lawyer but she loved to create in her spare time. Andreea often asked her why she didn't quit law and take up painting full time. Her dad made more than enough money to support the both of them, and she was sure her mother's works could be sold for quite a bit if she could get them into a gallery.

"You should never commodify your hobbies unless absolutely necessary Andreea. If you do you will no longer have anything to do for enjoyment, and certainly nothing to do for relaxation." That was her mothers favourite saying whenever the topic was brought up, and eventually Andreea just stopped mentioning it altogether.

She didn't think much about the room, she wasn't much of an artist herself and so had very little need to go into an art studio. Still, there were times when her hand would drift to the nob unknowingly and she would find herself turning it, trying to get in. Of course she knew there was no getting in. Her mother always kept the door locked and she wore the key around her neck on a small golden chain. Andreea had seen the key only a few times, but not in close enough detail to ever be able to draw it out or describe it to anyone.

-

It was one of those days now. Where Andreea found herself twisting the knob, trying to get into the room. She was in a sort of day dream, thinking about the cliffs at the end of their street that jutted down to touch the ocean.

"What have I told you Andreea? Really, the door again?"

"I-I didn't even realize." The words stuttered out of Andreea's mouth as she looked down at her hand in mid turn on the brass knob. She let go of it as though it were suddenly burning hot and starred down at her mother, "I swear."

Cecilia sighed looked at her with a kind and worried smile, "I know, why don't we go out to the cliffs? You always like that."

Andreea's panic had gone, and a smile now sat over her previously sunken lips.

-

The cliffs had always been Andreea's favourite place. Her parents would bring her to them every weekend and they would picnic and listen to the waves crash along the rocks below them while they watched the sun set. It had been months since they had been able to do it. Her father had been in the hospital with what her mother called shadows. She wasn't sure what it was, and the medical term was never given to her, shadows, that was all she knew. It had been what her mother had had when she had been sick during her second pregnancy. And what she had had at the same time, when she was five. She didn't remember it, she just knew that she felt frightened all the time. The fear, she assumed, must have been from how serious the illness was and the fact she was probably going to lose her mother to it at the same time she needed her most. Luckily, they had both survived the shadows and so she thought her father would most likely survive them as well. She thought about the shadows as her and her mother packed up a small basket with bread and cheese. She added in some grapes, and a bar of chocolate and her mother added in a bottle of wine for herself and some sparkling cider for Andreea. They wrapped their scarves around themselves to keep warm from the winds and made their way up the street towards the cliffs. When they had reached the end of the street they pulled back the large ferns that covered the path and followed the small gravel trail to the open grass along the rock face. It was warm. A beautiful summer evening in late July and the sun had turned the sky a beautiful mix of orange and pinks. The wind was mild and southern, but the scarves were kept on. They sat there for awhile in silence, starring out at the water and eating their dinner in quiet company.

"Andreea," Cecilia looked at her, a seriousness had touched her brow.

"Yes?"

Her mother had her hands in her lap and was picking at the skin that surrounded her perfectly manicured nails. A habit Andreea had never noticed but now that she looked closely seemed to have ravaged her mothers fingers for at least the past few days.

"Mom? What is it?"

"What do you remember about when you were sick? About the shadows?"

"Nothing really. I just remember feeling frightened all the time."

"Did you know they were the reason we bought this house?"

Of course Cecilia knew her daughter didn't know that, she knew that Andreea really don't know anything about the shadows or what they had cost them. If she was being honest Cecilia herself didn't know much more than her daughter did, at least not about what they were. She unfortunately knew more about what they did and what they were capable of. Andreea shook her head, no.

"After I lost your brother, I refused to go back to our old house, I thought that there were monsters that lived there and that they would keep hurting me. I was scared that one day

they might start hurting you. So we moved, do you remember that?"

"I remember daddy telling me to pack. And coming here almost the next day, and uncle John and aunt Seline staying with us while you got better."

"Good, you do remember. When we moved here I thought they would go away. And for a while they did, but as soon as I was better they came back. And they started to follow you around the house, that was when you got sick. The shadows, they made you sick Andreea. The doctors didn't know what to do and neither did I. We thought you were going to die. I stayed awake for weeks, I was so scared of losing you. Eventually your father started putting sleeping pills in my water just to get me to sleep for even a few hours. I used to have this really awful dream before your father was around and it stopped for awhile until I was pregnant with you and then I started to have it again until I was pregnant with your brother. Once we lost him the dreams disappeared to. When you were sick the dreams came back but this time they were slightly different. I won't burden you with the details of them, but at the end of the dream instead of waking up I turned around. It was something I had never done before. The world behind me was the same as the one in front of me, a perfect mirror, aside from a small lump on the ground a few yards in front of me. I went to it and on top of the dirt was a locket."

Cecilia pulled a small golden locket out of her pocket and handed it to Andreea. Andreea turned it over, inspecting it. She put her nail in the small groove on the size and meant to open it but before she could her mother grabbed her hand and closed it tightly. The locket dug into her palm and she pulled away. Her mother seemed to be unaware that she had squeezed too tight.

"This was the locket in my dreams. My mother gave it to me before she died and I it was one of the few possession I took with me when I left the farm. When I woke up from my

dream I had this sudden clarity that I needed to place a photo of my old family inside the locket to keep the shadows at bay. When I did that, they stopped coming. I need you to know this because the locket has been calling to you, I know it has. I see you reaching for the door almost like you're in a trance. I think it's calling you because it knows they will come for you too. When they do I might not be here, so I want you to know about it. You have to place a photo inside, I don't know what yours will be, only you will know that when it's time. But you must keep it safe. As I have in it's special room, where it will continue to stay until you need it. Do you understand?"

She did. But there was one thing that didn't make sense to her.

"If this stops the shadows, why haven't you used it for daddy?"

The blame was unmistakable in her voice as she slammed the locket back into her mothers hand.

"I've tried. I've tried so many times. All I can think is that it only works for our blood line, and since your father and I don't share the same blood, my mothers locket can offer him no shelter from the shadows."

The blame dissipated quickly and Andreea saw the defeat in her mothers eyes. They both knew what as coming, and for her mother, sometimes Andreea felt like her father was all she had.

Part Three

Chapter 1

things seen in the corner

It hadn't always been there, the thing in the corner of the room. It started when Shelly was born and when Andreea, her mother had gotten sick. Aki had told her it was all in her head, probably a post-partum symptom he said too many times to count. But Cosmina knew better. She knew that there were things that went bump in the night, her own mother had told her enough about them. Then there was the fact she could see the ghosts on the street that it seemed no one else could. She had always believed that the dead were still here, her mother and her grandparents had made sure she did. Despite that, she still went to have herself examined for any possible condition that made a person believe they could see ghosts at her husband's insistence. She also knew she wouldn't be diagnosed with anything, and she wasn't. Still, Aki refused to believe in the cowboy she saw with the bullet hole through him or the old Japanese woman in the 1950s housewife dress and apron who used to wander around her house when she was a little girl. She didn't even really mind that he didn't believe her or couldn't see what she saw when it came to the ghosts, but the thing in the corner of the room was different. Her mother had always told her there were worse things than ghosts, that ghosts couldn't touch the living and therefore couldn't hurt them. This Cosmina also knew. It had taken her some time to get used to but eventually, she did and when she was almost ten years old she finally came to terms with the fact that ghosts were going to be an everyday part of her life.

The thing in the corner, however, had not been an everyday part of her life. She had lived twenty-four years without ever seeing it. She had even started to think maybe her mother was a tad bit out there when she would go into one of her episodes and send Cosmina to her room, claiming there were bad things coming and she needed to go away. When Andreea had gotten sick, nothing overly serious the doctors had said even though they weren't quite sure what it was and still didn't know, Cosmina started to see black shadows rush by from the corners of her eyes. They seemed to circle her constantly but when she tried to stop and focus on them they'd be gone. Three months later she gave birth to Shelly and spent two blissful weeks with her before the thing in the corner appeared. She had tried to draw it for Aki so he could at least try and see what she saw, but no matter how many times she touched charcoal, pen, or pencil to paper, she couldn't get it right.

It had no face, no body, no anything. It was a looming darkness that hung in the corner of the room opposite Shelly's crib. In some ways, it seemed to have the outline of a man while also contorting into different shapes and sizes. There were no eyes where Cosmina had assumed they should be but still it watched her, and it waited. It never moved from the corner of the room and was there in the darkness and the light of the day. Cosmina actually preferred it in the darkness, she could still see it but it blended into the night that crept up around it. In the daylight, it was in stark contrast to the sunbeams that shone on it through the window. She hadn't understood how her husband couldn't see it. It seemed to absorb the light and refract it back at her with a wanting sort of sickness.

The day it moved to the corner over Shelly's crib Cosmina begged her husband to move. To let them go anywhere else but where they were.

"Aki, please. I know you don't believe me but it isn't for me. It's for Shelly, please she isn't safe."

Aki sat beside his wife on the bed and hung his head in despair. He took her hands in his and pressed them to his lips before looking up at her.

"My love. I believe that you see something, but the doctors said-"

"Screw the doctors!" Cosmina tore her hands away from her husband and looked at the darkness as it watched the two of them.

Aki took a steadying breath, "the doctors said this could be a part of your postpartum symptoms, seeing things that aren't there, worrying for our safety. It would make sense. Your mom didn't have an easy birth with you either, so it seems perfectly reasonable that you're struggling with Shelly."

Cosmina walked to the window, keeping her eye on the corner of the room as she did it. She had begun to spend all of her time in the room and would only leave it if Aki promised to stay and watch Shelly in the crib. At first, she had tried moving it, but no matter where she moved it to, the being followed, so she had put it back in the corner and now watch the thing that watched her and her daughter.

"There's something in this house Aki. I know you can't see it, or feel it, but it's there."

Aki looked to the corner above the crib where Cosmina seemed to fall asleep looking, "is it there now."

Cosmina let out a long sigh and ran her hands over her face and back into her hair, "it's always there Aki. Always. I'm not asking you anymore. I know we said we would do this on our own, but rents going up, and my parents have offered us the apartment downtown at the end of the month when the old tenants leave. I'm going, I'm getting away from that thing," she pointed above the crib and shuttered at the grin she received back from it, "and I'm going with or without you. But Shelly will be coming with me."

Now Aki was standing and it became more apparent to him that whatever his wife was going through was far more concerning than he had previously thought. He walked over to the window to stand beside her and placed a hand on her shoulder that she tried to shy away from. He dropped his hand

and reached for hers instead, which she let him do and loosely curled her fingers around his.

"Can't we talk about this first?"

"No. We can't. Either you come or you don't."

"Of course you know I'll follow you anywhere." He ran his thumb over the edge of her hand and she leaned into him, feeling his warmth.

She looked back over her shoulder toward the corner of the room where her child and its unwanted companion still sat, "I'm just hoping you're the only one who will."

Chapter 2

safety in fleeing

Cosmina loved her new home and loved that her husband and her daughter did too. Nearly twenty years they had spent here and nothing had shown up in the corner of the rooms, her dreams had finally stopped, and Shelly said she could feel the ghosts Cosmina saw but that she wasn't able to see them. She had thought that Shelly not being able to see them would make her uneasy, but after the trip to her families farm when Shelly was a little girl who came back terrified of the things her own mother called shadows that lived in the forest, she felt better knowing Shelly hadn't seen anything like that since.

One thing that had worried her since that trip though was her husband's sudden change in attitude towards the things she told him she saw. She had never given up on trying to make him believe and thought that if he did they would be that much stronger together. She never felt like he thought she was crazy or worried he might one day have enough, so she kept on with her stories of telling him of all the most unique dead things they passed on the street. In return he would tell say something like the brain of an artist is a magical thing, it makes even the craziest sorts of things seem plausible even when they're not or her personal favourite if you stop for a moment to breathe then there's a rational explanation for her, everything is explainable. Of course, he knew she wouldn't listen to him and she appreciated that he never pressed the issue. But when they returned from the trip it stopped. There were no more logical reasonings or moments where he tried to get her to see that ghosts weren't real and she most likely had an overactive imagination. Now it seemed he almost believed her. If she mentioned seeing someone she thought was worth mentioning he would stop and stare at the place she was pointing to, squinting as if trying to see passed whatever it was that wasn't allowing him into her version of the world.

"Hey hun," Aki walked into the living room and kissed his wife on the head while he laid his jacket over the back of the chair.

"Hi," Cosmina kissed the air absent-mindedly and continued on her drawing for her latest client, a large serpent tattoo that would cover their leg surrounded by Hello Kitty flowers.

Aki leaned over his wife and rested his head on hers, "that's interesting."

"People are so strange, the things they come up with. I love it, but I wish I could get inside their heads or spend a day with them, like how do they come up with this?" She gestured to the drawing with her pencil.

"People are strange says the ghost lady, all right," Aki laughed and Cosmina let out a small chuckle alongside him, speaking of strange people, did Shelly tell you about her dream last night?"

Cosmina froze. She stopped what she was doing and put down her drawing pad then turned herself to face Aki, "no? She's never been one for dreaming."

"That's what I thought too, which always seemed so strange given the sorts of things you two seem to be into. The ghosts and stuff."

Cosmina rolled her eyes and moved her hand in a continue sort of motion.

"Anyways, when we were having coffee this morning she told me she had the strangest dream. She was in a desert and there were these large plateaus all around her. She said the sand was this sort of bright orange colour, like those pictures you see of Idaho or something, and every time she tried to step forward it would only move her a step backward until the cowboy showed up."

At the mention of the cowboy, Cosmina went completely still, "what cowboy?"

"She said that it was some cowboy you had told her about. This sort of old-timey guy with these crazy spurs and a cigar and a bullet hole that went right through him. He rode up to her on a horse and walked over to her, crushed his cigar with his foot, and gave her this really sad look then got on his horse and walked away. It's nothing like crazy, but she's never really mentioned dreaming before and she described it in this really intense detail that I'm not doing justice. I thought she would have mentioned it to you, she said it seemed like she was actually there and asked if I thought that was possible. That's the sort of thing I would've asked you if I were her."

Cosmina looked up as if she could somehow see through the ceiling and up into her daughter's room, "it was probably nothing."

"Really?" Aki was shocked, she always thought there was something to be deciphered from a dream and it concerned him that she was brushing this one off, "I thought-"

"Look, it's probably nothing. So leave it." She snapped and as she did it she hung her head with regret, he didn't deserve for her to shut him out.

Aki looked knowingly at her and walked around the couch to take a seat beside her. She leaned into him and rested her head on his shoulder and let out a weary sigh.

"We need to move Aki."

"Move. Why? Are you seeing that thing again?"

"No. Do you remember about three years ago when Shelly mentioned that man in the blue jacket and I told her it was just the heebie jeebies?"

"The man in the blue jacket...." Aki contemplated it a moment, trying hard to recall the memory, "oh yes, the one in the alleyway she said made her so uneasy."

"Yes, well, it wasn't just a man in some jacket that happened to look up at her. It was one of them, and she told

me she couldn't see them. I believe her about that, she hasn't seemed like she's noticed them when I have but she says she can feel them and there's no reason for her to lie. But she saw him. I knew him, before all of this when he was just a man and not some version of him made out of his soul or matter or whatever it is that makes them what they are. I didn't even think he really had much of a soul, so I would doubt if it's that," the tone of her voice had turned bitter and tears had begun to tighten around her vocal cords, "he used to teach at my old high school. I was in his class in my grade ten year and there was this group of boys that would not leave me alone. One minute they were catcalling me and trying to get me to come out to their lake house with them, the next they were calling me all these slurs and saying the most racist, creepy bullshit. They were in his class with me and he never said anything to them so I assumed he agreed with their sentiments and left it at that. Then we went on this field trip, the one that goes to Victoria, did your school ever do that?"

"We didn't but I know the one you mean," he had a feeling he knew where the story was going and couldn't bring himself to look anywhere but dead ahead, letting his vision glaze over.

All Cosmina did was nod, her head still resting on him. She reached for his hand and he slipped his fingers between hers, squeezing her hand to assure her he wasn't going anywhere and she wasn't alone.

Cosmina continued, "we were on the field trip and he was one of the chaperones. I went to grab some ice that just so happened to be across the hall from those assholes' room and I don't know how they knew I was there but they came out and cornered me. I tried to push past them but they shoved me and the one just slammed his hand over my mouth and banged my head off the ice machine. I bit him but he wouldn't pull away. Then they just started screaming at me. How people like me didn't belong there which made me laugh and I shouldn't have laughed but I couldn't help him. They started talking about all these things they were going to do to me and I was so scared and I was kicking and trying to push them away. But every time I tried to move I'd get another shove or another bash of my head or a boot to the shins. Then my teacher walked by, and he just looked at me for a moment. I remember just looking at him, begging him to make them stop. They felt so sure of themselves with him that they didn't even turn around until he put his arm on one of their shoulders and told them it was enough. You should have seen it, the way he did it. It was like he was a proud father telling his son to stop scoring when the other team is down by ten. They let me go and went back to their room and he asked me what happened. I told him and all he said was you must have provoked them in some way, and you know you're not supposed to leave your room unaccompanied, girls need to be more careful of the positions they put themselves in. Then he sent me back to my room. And I know he's wrong, but part of me feels like maybe he wasn't. I knew I wasn't supposed to go down there alone or anywhere alone but I wasn't really friends with the girl in my room and my friends were at some political seminar thing that I wasn't interested in. I knew that they were out to get me and I should have been more careful."

Aki gently slid his shoulder out from under her and grabbed her chin, tilting her head up to his face, "none of that was your fault. None of it."

"I know," she averted her gaze back to the stained grey fabric of the scratchy sofa she had been meaning to replace, "I know. That's not even the part that gets me. I honestly got over it pretty quickly."

"That's concerning."

Cosmina waved him off and continued with his story, still not looking at him. She was too ashamed to tell him that she still cried about that night. It was easier to tell him and to tell herself that she was over it and it could have been worse, that they rouged her up a bit but other women suffered more and she didn't have much right to hold onto something so small with such a heavy weight.

"He died the next year, in a car accident. And I was happy. I was so happy. My friends and I threw this huge party at my house and we didn't tell anyone what it was for but we knew. I blacked out about halfway through and when I woke up the house was trashed. When my parents got home they were pissed and I remember the look on my mom's face. Pure disappointment. She knew I hated him and knew he died and she wasn't naive so it didn't take her long to figure out what the party had been in honour of."

"That surprises me. I didn't think she would be one to overlook something like that."

"As I said, I moved on from it pretty quickly and I didn't want to burden her with it so she didn't know. She just thought I was throwing a party because some teacher who was a dick to me was dead. And I let her think it. I hadn't ever seen him so I thought that maybe he hadn't stuck around and that was fine with me. But the man that Shelly described that night, that was him. He always wore that stupid blue jacket and I hated it. I don't even know why I hated it, it was just so bright and obnoxious and it made me hate him even more. I even laughed when I found out that's what he had been wearing when he died. It was just so ironic and I couldn't help myself. But it worried me that he was watching Shelly and I had thought about moving then but she never mentioned seeing him again and I thought that was the end of things. But those dreams never mean anything good. I used to have them too, and so did my mom, and my grandmother. My grandfather even used to have them occasionally, his were different though, he dreamt of this large forest. He used to tell me about it, it was covered in giant pine trees that stretched all the way to the ocean and in the distance, down the coast he used to see this village burning and every time he would try and run towards it, it would send

him further backward. Mine was like Shelly's though but I never saw a cowboy, I never saw anyone. But I was in the same place. This vast desert with Idaho sands and giant plateaus was something I dreamt about right before my mom got sick and Shelly was born. But in mine, there was this crazy rain storm and a flash flood and the waters would rush toward me and I would try to run away but I couldn't turn around and then I was drowning, then I would wake up."

"So you want to move because Shelly is having strange dreams? That hardly seems like grounds for moving Cos."

"You don't understand," she put her head in her hands and spoke in a muffled half whisper, "that's when they start to come. Whatever that thing was in the room, it was the same thing my mom used to see."

"Okay," Aki stopped her from continuing, that had been all he needed to hear to send his mind back to that day in Andreea's kitchen, "where were you thinking?"

She sat up and looked at him, surprised it had been that quick. She thought it would take longer. Days, if not weeks of pleading had been planned out to convince him to leave with her, to run.

"The Gulf Islands."

Chapter 3

running

Cosmina felt terrible lying to Shelly. Telling her that she was stuck in meetings with clients who wanted larger, more elaborate designs than she had previously done while sneaking off to meet with her realtor while Aki hosted viewings of their apartment on days they knew Shelly had plans to be gone. It all felt wrong. They weren't a family of many secrets, some, to protect Shelly, but until now Cosmina hadn't thought they were ever a family who would do something like this, and yet here they were.

She leaned over the railing of the ferry as she took in the beauty of the small islands they had begun to sail through. The way the light twinkled off the waves and lit up the lush greens of the coastal rainforests. She watched as a whale breached in the distance and thought about the trip she had taken to Salt Spring with her own parents when she was younger. That trip was part of the reason she had chosen this place. When she was here she had felt safe, it was the only time in her life she had ever felt that fully. There was no itching at the back of her mind that something was creeping up on her, nothing that made her feel like she had to keep running.

The horn blasted to signal they were coming into the terminal and pulled her out of her thoughts and back to the task at hand; viewing their potential new home.

-

The drive was longer than the realtor had said, but she didn't mind, after all, she had grown up on a farm where the drive to town for groceries had been double what this was. Plus, she enjoyed driving, it cleared her head. She drove in silence as she took in the vast forests and the twinkling waters that occasionally peaked through the cracks. Fernwood, that was her destination, at the far end of the island. She thought about the pictures the realtor had shown her, if Shelly would hate her for moving her here, or worse if Shelly would choose to stay behind. After all, she was an adult now and had been talking about moving out and living on her own while she figured out what she wanted to do in life. Cosmina and Aki had never pushed the issue much, they believed education was important but didn't want Shelly to go if it wasn't something she was interested in, and she got enough education on her own through books and academic papers she seemed to like reading on her spare time with Aki. She was sure Shelly would come with them when she had originally brought up the point of moving but now she wasn't sure. She had started to doubt herself and as she drove it only got worse. She began to notice how little of anything there was besides forest and water and more forest with the odd house cut out from it. Of course, there were small communities and a larger centre of the main town, but Shelly had never lived in a place so secluded before. And when they visited the farm Shelly was always ready to head back to the city within a week.

Cosmina shook her head, trying to shake the worry right out of herself. She reminded herself of Shelly's well being, told herself that they all needed to leave. She thought of how different her daughter had seemed over the last few months. Her face had become paler it seemed, like the colour was being drained from her, the way it did when she was sick. She spent less time with her friends and more time in the confines of her own bedroom and bags had appeared under her eyes as though she had stopped sleeping. She knew for a fact that Shelly had been sleeping less, she heard her at night, pacing around her room or wandering around in the living room of their apartment. What she thought was odd wasn't the fact that Shelly couldn't sleep, she had always struggled with it, but it was the fact she didn't seem to be doing anything. Aki often had to get up and ask Shelly to turn down the music, or the TV when she started her nightly routine of waking and wandering. But now there was nothing, no noise, no light creeping under their door, Shelly had just been wandering around in the dark, as though she were hiding from something, and that worried Cosmina. Pairing that with the dark circles that ringed her eyes and meant she had been sleeping even less than before heightened that concern.

She let out a cautious breath as she rounded what seemed to be the last corner according to her phone screen that had been set to a map of her drive.

"This is what's best for Shelly," she spoke out loud to herself, as though that would make it true.

When she exited her car, the realtor hers had put her in contact with on the island was waiting at the front door of the house. Cosmina looked around and almost instantly her worries seemed to go away. The house was beautiful and everything she hoped it would be. The pictures hadn't done it justice and even those had made her fall in love with it. They toured the house and the grounds before getting into the realtor's car for her to show Cosmina around the rest of the island.

"So, what made your family decide to move to Salt Spring?"

Cosmina had been texting her husband and it took her a moment to register what the realtor had asked her, "hm? Oh. We needed a break, a place where we could get away from everything."

"I hear ya. That's why I moved her a couple of years ago. I went through this nasty divorce and we didn't have any kids to keep me in the city with him, so I thought I might try and eat pray love my way out of the sadness by moving to an island. I know it's not exactly a tropical paradise but it feels a bit like paradise when you're running from something."

Cosmina didn't usually mind talkative people, she actually preferred it in her line of work, but she wanted nothing more than for the realtor to shut up. But when she said that last bit, that it felt like paradise when you were running from something it struck something in her.

"We'd like to put in an offer."

"Really?" The realtor took her eyes off the road a moment to look at Cosmina with surprise before composing herself and looking back out at the road, "I'm not surprised, it's such a beautiful place, but people don't usually want to move here in the winter. This," she gestured to the forest and the bright sun that glared down in front of them, "is unusual for this time of year. You're obviously used to the rain in Vancouver but it gets stormy here, and cold. I'm not trying to talk you out of it by any means, I'm just surprised you were interested in moving at this time of year to begin with is all. You know when your realtor, what was her name, Marlene? Yeah, that was it, when Marlene called me and said she wanted to set up a viewing I nearly fell out of my chair. I had been so bored, no one ever wants to buy in the winter so I'm pretty much a social media influencer during that time, posting about houses and listings to drum up business for the spring."

Cosmina waited only half patiently for her to finish talking while she texted Aki that she was putting in an offer on the house and to get serious with the open houses since she was sure their offer would be excepted. They pulled up to a small coffee shop in the middle of the town that Cosmina hadn't even realized they had entered.

"We can go over numbers and everything else over coffee if you're up for it," the realtor looked at her with a hopeful sort of cheer that made Cosmina think of a puppy begging for you to love it.

Cosmina smiled at her and put her phone away, "yes, sorry, I just had to check with my husband that we were on the same page. I'm all ears and coffee sounds great."

The coffee shop was a quint space with walls lined from floor to ceiling with various paintings and photographs listed for sale by local artists. She thought of Aki and how his work could be featured on the walls for tourists to spend too much money on while they ate their butter scones and sipped their lattes. Plants hung from large wood beams in the roof that tied together nicely with the mismatched thrifted chairs and coffee tables that served as the seating.

She ordered a cappuccino and so did the realtor before they sat down to go over the details of the sale and the price they were willing to offer, which the owner accepted as soon as the realtor called him.

"It's official," she clapped with her phone still in her hands and nearly bounced out of her chair, "my client accepted your offer. We're excited to have you on the island."

There of course were still the legal documents and the actual paperwork and financial details that needed to be worked out and Cosmina realized she should call her realtor on the mainland and fill her in. She asked the realtor to excuse her for a moment while she called Marlene and discussed how to proceed on that her end.

By the time Cosmina was back on the ferry and heading home to her family's apartment for the last time, Aki had received three offers on their home. She didn't know how he had done it but he had gotten nearly $50,000 over their asking price which set them at a much larger budget for renovations and anything extra that they might want to do to their new home. Cosmina had lowballed the house in Fernwood and was willing to pay over the asking price if the negotiations went that way, she had actually gone there with the idea of offering over the asking price. But when the realtor started talking about how hard it was to sell during this time of year, and considering that the house had been on the market for nearly a year, she decided to see what a lowball price might get her, and to her surprise, it got her everything she had wanted.

Chapter 4

paradise

Everything was perfect. Shelly was making new friends, one of whom Cosmina suspected might be something more than a friend, she and Aki were happier than they had ever been, he was painting and with tourism starting her shop had been booked into overtime nearly every day. The house was gorgeous and the yard was incredible. She hadn't realized how much she had missed having land and space between her and her neighbours until she had it back again. Jibbles and Edward seemed to be happy here as well and were getting along with one another better than she had thought they would. The storms in the winter had gotten the family down on a few occasions when their bodies and minds started to miss the sun, but more often than not they sat in their living room with the fire roaring and watched the lightning flash over the water and the cracked the windows to hear the thunder and the crash of the waves as they slammed into the rock face below.

Shelly hadn't mentioned any more dreams to her or her husband, and she hadn't seen a single ghost since they arrived. This was a place they could stay in forever, Shelly even seemed to be happy enough here that Cosmina thought she might stay forever too. She had hoped she would, that she would learn to be safe around the things that seemed to haunt her family, that she would learn how to run from them, how to hide and keep them from following.

-

She thought about her contentment and the happiness they all seemed to feel here as she ran her needle over another tourist's skin, tracing the outline of a sea turtle for the hundredth time. She didn't mind the basic tourist tattoos that they pointed out in her pre-drawn book for walk-ins. She had enough clients from the city and some new ones here that loved her work enough to get custom pieces so the tourists getting some small symbol to remember their trip wasn't as mind-numbing as other artists had made it out to be.

"Hey Cos," Amy, her apprentice approached her cautiously, a look of worry on her face.

She never bothered Cosmina during an appointment, never.

Cosmina's heart started to pound and she had to put down her machine before her hand started shaking. She waited for Amy to tell her what was going on, she thought if she opened her mouth to speak there might not be anything that came out, so waiting was the best bet.

"Your husband just called. Shelly's in the hospital."

"What? Is it serious? What did he say?" The words spilled out of her, sound could still come from her after all, and the panic was clear in it.

"I don't know, he sounded worried and said you needed to be there."

"Oh my god," she whispered it to herself while wiping down her station and sterilizing what needed to be done.

"Amber," she addressed the woman who was getting the turtle tattooed on her right calf, "this is Amy, she's an apprentice here. If you're okay with it she can finish your tattoo or I can book you in for an appointment later this evening to finish it."

Amber shifted, twisting to look at Cosmina, "Amy can finish it. I hope everything's okay."

"I hope so too, she got up and grabbed her keys from her desk then turned back to Amy, "call and cancel all of my appointments, tell them you can take them if they would like and if not I will call them when I know more and reschedule."

Amy nodded and told Cosmina not to worry, that she would lock up and take care of everything, and that she hoped Shelly was okay.

So much for perfect. She raced to her car and sped all the way through town to get to the hospital, ignoring the possibility of a ticket. When she pulled into the parking lot she saw Marcus's car parked beside the one he and his husband had let her husband borrow until he bought his own. She swung into an empty stall, nearly clipping the mirror of the car beside her and threw the car into park. The doors nearly hit her, or she nearly hit them as she rushed into the hospital at a dead sprint and only slowed when the automatic doors didn't open at her pace. When she turned the corner into the lobby she saw Sam seated in a chair, wrapped in a thick grey blanket and covered in bandages with Tom sitting next to her in silence, his leg bouncing fiercely as he picked at his nails, eyes focused on the floor. Aki stood with Marcus and Izac, their faces flushed with worry and confusion. She half walked half jogged over to them, watching Sam as she did. Sam didn't notice her, or if she did she made no indication of it, and Tom glanced at her for only a moment before looking back to the floor.

"What happened?"

The men turned to look at her and Marcus and Izac made their way to the side so she could speak to Aki privately. She watched as they went over to Tom and Marcus jutted his chin toward the end of the hallway, telling Tom they needed to speak away from everyone. Even when Tom moved Sam didn't look up from the floor and something about that made Cosmina's heart beat even faster.

"There was some kind of incident. In the forest."

"What kind of incident?" Cosmina didn't like the lack of information her husband was giving her or the hushed tones that Tom seemed to be speaking in with his uncles.

"We aren't really sure. Sam won't speak and Tom said he found them on the side of the road by the forest but he doesn't know anything either. He said he dropped Edward off at the vet before they got here and he was in pretty bad shape."

Cosmina heard whispering from the front desk and turned to see a police officer speaking to two nurses and the three of them kept glancing toward the end of the hall where Tom stood with Marcus and Izac. How had she not noticed the policeman before, and why was he here?

"Why are the police involved?"

"Apparently the nurses thought Tom was suspicious, and under the circumstances and the conditions he brought the girls in they thought it best to call the cops."

Cosmina nodded her head and looked past the policeman toward the double doors that led back into the operating rooms that had just swung open. A nurse wheeled Shelly out with a brace now wrapped around her ankle and her doctor followed closely behind. Cosmina wanted to run to her, to hold her and kiss her and never let her go. To see Shelly in this condition scared her and she felt her stomach drop at the realization that this was no longer a place where she never felt fear. Before she could take a step Aki grabbed her elbow and gently guided her to look at Sam who had finally broken out of her trance and looked up at Shelly.

Aki whispered in her ear, "just leave them be a moment."

"Fine, but I want answers."

She pulled Aki toward the doctor and the nurse who were now consulting with the officer and the two nurses at the front desk. When they looked up at her she demanded to know what had happened to Shelly and Sam and what was wrong with Shelly's ankle. The doctor filled her and Aki in on everything they knew so far and the officer informed her that he would be questioning the kids and assured her not to worry, that he would be conducting a thorough investigation into Tom as well. She couldn't understand why they all seemed to be acting like Tom was so guilty of something. He had taken Edward to the vet and brought the girls to the hospital. He was Sam's cousin and the girls' friend, he had helped them and yet the entire hospital was acting like he was some kind of criminal.

"The girls seemed scared of him miss," the officer answered as if reading her mind.

"Scared? Of Tom?"

"That's what the nurses have told me."

The nurses nodded and confirmed. She looked back at Tom who was hugging Shelly and receiving the same level of affection back. That didn't seem like someone her daughter was scared of in her opinion.

▪

She was happy to see Sal and Kyra arrive to comfort Shelly. As soon as she knew Shelly was okay she texted them to let them know what had happened. Seeing how happy it made Shelly to see their faces brightened her mood and she almost forgot about how worried she still was about the entire thing. When Shelly told her and Aki the story there were parts she seemed to be leaving out. Aki didn't think so but he had never been that good at telling when a person was lying, Cosmina on the other hand was. It took everything in her to leave and let the girls have their space. She wanted nothing more than to be by Shelly's side through every moment of her recovery, still, she knew that space and privacy was the best thing for the friends right now so she headed toward town.

She thought about Shelly's story as she drove and thought about the pieces of the story that seemed to be missing. There had to of been more that they saw in the woods than they had let on, and Marcus had told her that Sam refused to leave her room, and even more troubling, refused to see Tom. Both girls had assured their parents that Tom had nothing to do with it, and while Cosmina believed he had nothing to do with the harm they suffered, she didn't believe that he had nothing to do with it.

She stopped the car and swung it around to drive back the way she had come. She knew that the place was a lie, that much was clear, they never went into the woods down the road they had told the cop, and they never went into the woods behind their houses either, but something told her that they had. That the place they had been was close to home. She drove to the end of the road where the trees thinned ever so slightly and a small deer trail led up into the woods. It had always seemed strange that they lived so close to this yet the kids never hiked there even when they took Edward. The forest here seemed just as beautiful as any on the island and tourists were constantly parking near their driveway in the warmer months to trek through the trails that twisted and turned up behind their homes.

She sat there a moment, looking into the woods, her foot on the brake and the car idling. Her heart pounded. There was nothing out of the ordinary that she could see but the hairs on the back of her neck were now standing up and a feeling of terror started to rise in her. She leaned forward, thinking maybe she might see something if she got another two inches closer. And she did. Something tore through the forest too fast for her to see what it was and suddenly her ears were pierced with a growling sort of squeal. The thing was on the other side of her car now, tearing through the trees, the sound growing louder. Her heart felt like it would beat out of her chest. Then the car was in reverse and she was spinning, she pushed the gear shift into drive and slammed her foot into the gas, taking off again towards town. She wanted to go home, to see Shelly, to ask her about what she saw in the woods, but something in her told her not to, not yet, it wasn't time.

▪

When she finally got home Kyra's vehicle was nowhere to be found and Tom's truck was in the driveway. She thought that the girls might have gone to town and asked Tom to watch the dog or maybe he had come to meet Shelly's friends and one of them took the car out for something. She walked inside quietly and listened, the sound of Shelly and Tom's voices travelled to the door from the kitchen. She walked in as though she hadn't noticed a single thing odd about the situation, no Kyra or Sal,

Tom and Shelly hugging with an air of tension filling the room around them.

"Oop! Sorry, I didn't mean to interrupt," she thought she played it off quite well.

Shelly and Tom hurriedly untangled themselves and assured her that she hadn't interrupted anything to which she raised an internal eyebrow. Then the two moved out of the kitchen and took Edward for his rehabilitation walk. Cosmina winced every time he moved, they all loved the dog, he was kind and loving and loyal, all the things Shelly wanted him to be, and to see him in so much pain broke her heart.

She put the groceries away, humming to herself. She was still shaken from the thing she saw in the woods and the fact that Shelly's friends seemed to pack up and leave for a reason she couldn't figure out. So she hummed to calm herself, a low tune to the sound of a song her grandmother used to sing to her when they would bake together.

Then the phone rang.

She looked at the name on the screen DAD. Her stomach dropped, he never called her.

She let it ring until the last second before cautiously answering.

"Hello?" The word took a moment to leave her lips.

"Hi dear," her father sounded as though he had been crying, she couldn't remember the last time he had sounded like that.

"Dad," she paused, "what's going on?"

His breath caught and she thought she could feel his tears seeping through the phone and wetting her cheeks. She reached up to touch her face and realized the tears were her own.

"Your mother. She's gone."

It was all he could manage to say she's gone. Cosmina wanted to comfort him, to tell him she loved him and talk to him about what had happened, but she knew what had happened, and all she could do was end the call.

She stood staring at the phone, waiting for him to call her back and tell her he had misspoke, that her mother was in the hospital but she was okay, she was alive. She knew it wasn't coming, knew that what he said was real and that she was gone. A feeling had crept up in her when the thing in the woods had begun its wail, not just terror but an immense loneliness, and now she believe that part of her knew this was coming.

Her head shot up at the sound of nails tapping on the floor rushing toward her. She let out a breath of relief when she came out of her head and realized the sound had only been Edward and her family.

"I need to tell you guys something," Shelly broke the silence.

Cosmina hadn't been prepared for Shelly to tell them she was gay, not that she cared nor was she surprised, and she felt slightly ashamed that her automatic assumption was for Shelly and Tom to be secretly seeing each other. She felt even more ashamed that all she could do was pace and drum her fingers on her legs as Shelly tried to explain to her and her husband how she defined herself and what that meant. Cosmina only half heard it, she wanted to, tried to, but she couldn't and the harder she tried the more she felt like she was going to burst, and she did. She collapsed into her husband's lap and the tears began to stream down her face in uncontrollable waves.

"I'm so sorry Shelly this has nothing to do with what you just told us," her voice was muffled against Aki's legs and it took everything in her to get the words out.

He rubbed her back and tried to get her to sit up and explain what was going on. It took her several tries. Each time she looked at Shelly the tears started up again.

"I got a call… when you were outside with Tom. My… my mom…" she choked on the words, "she's gone. They took her. And she's gone."

Aki rubbed her back as she dropped her head back into his lap, "what do you mean? They took her? Whose they?"

Cosmina wanted to explain to him, to tell him that she knew that the thing in the corner and those things in the woods were what had taken her, that she didn't have anything to justify what she was saying but that she knew. And the part of her that she had been ignoring for so long, the part of her that felt how similar her daughter was to her in all the wrong ways, knew that Shelly knew as well.

She sat up and blinked the tears out of her eyes, the house seemed to be dimmer all of a sudden and she could hear the yip of a coyote pack in the distance, which Edward responded to with a low growl. When the tears cleared she looked at Shelly and all she could do was scream. They were surrounding her, the shadows that had plagued their first home, her mother, her grandmother. They clung to her, grabbing at her with non-existent hands and with faceless smiles that smirked at her as though taunting her for trying to run, the ripped Shelly off the couch.

Chapter 5

the locket

All she could do was scream as she flailed her arms and legs wildly, trying to break free from the darkness that was pulling her toward the open patio door. She screamed until her air supply was cut. Something was grabbing her throat but when she clawed at it she only managed to carve long gashes into her own skin.

Edward tried his best to rush to her but was knocked aside by the dark figures that seemed to be engulfing her. He lay still on the ground and whimpered, she tried to call to him but her throat was being crushed and the edges of her vision had started to fade.

She looked wildly around the room, trying to find her parents. Her mother was frozen on the couch where she had been. She was screaming something, yelling toward her but the oxygen was fading and the voice seemed to be lost to her. Then she heard the door behind her slam shut and suddenly she was on the ground and the air was flooding back into her lungs. She gasped and choked on the sudden levels of oxygen that now sped their way through her. Edward made his way to his feet and limped toward her where her father was now holding her head in his lap.

"What was that!" Her father almost yelled it at her mother, demanding to know what had just happened.

Shelly knew she couldn't speak, could see she was frozen in place and that this had not been her mother's first encounter with the things that hid in the corners of the room.

"The things that took grandma," was all she could say.

-

Shelly and her mother sat side by side on her parent's bed, a blanket wrapped around their shoulders and mugs of warm tea in their hands. Jibbles was curled in her lap and Edward was stretched out beside the bed. Her father had carried him down for her and she thanked him over and over again for doing it. They decided that they would speak about what had happened in the morning and that for now, she would sleep in the bed with Cosmina, while Aki slept with Edward on the floor.

When they had finished their tea they crawled under the covers and placed their mugs on the nightstands. No one said a word and Cosmina turned the lights out with all of them still dressed in their clothes from the day. Shelly had never liked to sleep in her regular clothes, but tonight she couldn't stand the thought of being alone to change into anything else, so she left them on. She had to remind herself how to breathe, one breath in, one breath out. It was all she had thought of since she had been nearly drug out of the house by something her father couldn't even see, as far as she knew.

She jumped when her mother reached her arm up and wrapped it around her shoulder, pulling her into her chest. The two of them lay like that the entire night, neither one closing their eyes until sleep forced them to close and pulled them into their dreams.

▪

Shelly had hoped to see the cowboy that night but he was nowhere to be found. She was still in the desert, and now it seemed she was able to move freely around it, as long as she only went forward. She made her way toward the cave he had taken her to, hoping to find him there, but when she reached the base of the mountain the trail was gone. Then suddenly the dream started to change, the world shimmered and folded in on itself and when she could finally make sense of what she saw in front of her she was in a vast forest at the edge of a cliff that had been cut away by the raging ocean below. She looked out over the water toward a light in the distance and thought she could hear screaming.

Then someone grabbed her shoulder and she jumped as she spun around, catching her heel on the edge of the rock, then suddenly she was falling, and just as suddenly she stopped. Someone grabbed her around the arm and pulled her back onto solid ground. She looked up at him, an olive-skinned man with kind eyes and a kinder smile.

"Shelly," his smile widened and relief spread over her face as he looked at her, "I've been looking for you. I'm-"

Shelly cut him off, "Andrei. You're my great grandpa Andrei, aren't you?"

He chuckled and looked down at her as she steadied herself, making sure she wasn't too close to the edge. He was a towering man that stood high above her, and someone who would have been intimidating if it weren't for his kind eyes.

"That I am," he said to her and turned to walk back into the forest, "come."

He didn't look back at her as he spoke and Shelly had to jog to catch up to him when she realized he wasn't going to wait.

They walked in silence, the only sounds were their footsteps which seemed to be absorbed into the forest around them. It reminded Shelly of the forest that surrounded her grandparent's place, large coniferous trees stretched to the sky, evergreen oaks created wide canopies that shielded them from the outside world and sturdy beech trees lit up the forest with red and yellow leaves that stood out in a striking burst of colours amidst the greens. A wild lynx with pointed tufts that jutted upwards from the tips of its ears, and paws large enough to be a bear trotted beside them beneath the cover of the trees. Shelly jumped when she noticed it but soon calmed when she saw how little attention Andrei paid to it. She thought back to the coyotes that had so recently plagued her and found an odd sense of calm when she looked at the wild cat that she had not felt before. They walked for what felt like hours. Shelly had so many questions she wanted to ask but something held her back from speaking, so she said nothing, just watched as the lynx snaked through the trees, occasionally taking her gaze to the ground when she stumbled over a root or a rock stuck tightly in the dirt.

Eventually, they came to a small part of the forest that had been cleared of debris, beneath a dense oak tree. Against its trunk sat a rolled-up blanket, and a suitcase. A little way to the left, still beneath the cover of the foliage were the remnants of a fire; burned stones situated in a circle, charred branches that hadn't burned all the way, and ashes.

Andrei made his way to the trunk of the tree, sitting himself down on a large root that stuck out from the forest floor. The lynx had made its way to the edge of the makeshift camp and sat, watching the two of them. Shelly followed suit and found a try patch of dirt and plopped herself down less gracefully than she had intended to.

"Is this your camp?"

He nodded, "it is."

"Where are we?"

"In a memory, my memory, one from a home that was lost a long time ago," he looked around the forest as he said it, and the kindness in his eyes faded to be replaced by a sad sort of longing that made Shelly feel homesick for somewhere she had never been.

"I don't understand. How can this be your memory if I've never even met you?"

"Memory works in interesting ways, Shelly. Ways I won't pretend to understand. But I shared this memory with your great-grandmother, Cecilia, and so it became a collective memory. And maybe it was passed from us into our daughter, then from her into your mother, and from your mother to you. That's the only way I've been able to make sense of any of it."

"Make sense of any of it? I'm sorry I don't really understand. Everyone keeps speaking to me in these riddles and I don't know what to make of them. I know you're only in

my dream, but I'm scared grandpa Andrei, I'm really scared to wake up."

He leaned over to her and rested his hand on her knee for comfort.

"My Cecilia used to see them to you know. She would tell me there were these dark things that would latch onto me and she was petrified of them, and the longer we were together the more frequent they became and then they started to come for her too," he started to cry at this, a soft sort of pain escaping him in small irregular droplets, "she lost me to them, and then your grandmother lost her. I never forgave myself for not telling her I saw them too."

His head hung in shame and Shelly couldn't believe what she had heard.

"You saw them too?"

He didn't answer, only nodded his head.

Shelly stood up and started to pace the campsite, then she was yelling, "you saw them too! And you never told her. You let her feel like she was alone in it all and then what? You never thought to help her?" She was practically screaming now.

Andrei just sat there, trying to think of the words that might calm her, that might help her understand. Eventually, he asked her to sit back down again and try to listen to what he had to say. She did so reluctantly.

"I couldn't see them the way she did, as the darkness that she saw. And I never was able to see them, as she described, when they were latched on. But I saw memories that haunted me, she would point to a corner of the room with a shaking finger speaking of shadows and I would turn to see a man in a Nazi uniform, I would see the members of the catholic church and old faces from neighbouring villages I had long since forgotten. I thought if I pretended, if I ran, like your mother, that I could make them go away."

Shelly stopped him, "what do you mean like my mother? She sees ghosts but she always told me they can't hurt people."

"In a way she's right, and in some ways, she's not. Ghosts can't hurt people. They can't touch us or speak to us unless they're like your mother, but some ghosts, ghosts that we hold in ourselves, those ones can hurt us. Those shadows your grandmother saw, that you see and that your mother so desperately tried to run from, those were like my shadows, some of them are mine. Do you understand what I mean?"

Shelly shook her head, "I don't know."

He smiled at her again, the sadness still in his eyes, mixing with what Shelly thought was hope, "I think you do."

The dream began to fade as the lynx made its way into the camp. It wrapped its body around Shelly and flicked its tail across her nose. She tried to stop it from ending, to grab hold of something, anything that might keep her there for just a little while longer. She needed more answers and Andrei seemed to have them.

▪

Jibbles flicked his tail across Shelly's face and she swiped at it, mumbling in her sleep as her mother shook her shoulder. She opened her eyes to her parents standing over her, worry contorted their faces in ways she almost couldn't look at.

"Are you okay Shelly Belly? We heard you talking to someone, asking them to stay, telling them you didn't understand."

"I was just dreaming, it was nothing."

"It wasn't nothing," it was her mother who spoke this time, "we need to talk about the dreams Shelly. Yours and mine," she dropped her gaze when she said mine.

"You've been having strange dreams too?" Shelly sat up now and her sense seemed to be fully waking up.

"Like I said, we need to talk."

Shelly looked to her father for clarification, but all he gave her was a smile and a kiss on the forehead. Her parents helped her to her room, the incident from the night before had made her ankle much worse and movements even harder than they had been. Cosmina helped her change into a loosely fitted dress that stopped just below the knees and drew attention to the chunky boot that held her ankle in place.

"I'm sorry," Shelly said as her mother shimmied the dress over her head.

"Why would you say that?"

Shelly wasn't sure why she had said it and wrapped her arms around her mother's shoulder instead of trying to find a reason. They stayed like that for a moment, Shelly pulling her mother into her chest as though protecting her from all the things Andrei had said she was running from.Cosmina pulled away before the tears could start and the two walked back to the hallway where Aki stood waiting to help Shelly up the stairs. It appeared he had already taken Edward up since he waited at the top of the stairs and started to wag his tail when Shelly came into view.

They all sat around the kitchen table with an open letter placed neatly in the centre. Edward lay at Shelly's feet and Jibbles had placed himself inconveniently on Cosmina's lap. Aki had made them all tea, for the nerves he said, and now the filled mugs sat beside them untouched and growing colder by the minute.

Shelly broke the silence and reached for the envelope, "what's this?"

Cosmina tried to hide the pain in her voice, "it's from your grandmother."

Shelly looked at the letter, scared of what she might find inside, as though the paper itself might jump out and bite her. Then she looked back at her parents.

"Have you read it yet?"

"No," it was Aki who answered, "but we opened it, and this was inside," he held up a golden locket.

"I tried to read it, but I just hear her voice. You don't have to try to either, your father said he would read it for us if we need."

Shelly shook her head, she wanted to at least try. She pulled out the letter and unfolded it.

To my darlings Cosmina and Shelly,

I'm sorry I won't be around to answer your questions by the time this letter reaches
you. They are coming for me, they have been for a long time and now it seems that
time has run out and the strength I once had has been taken from me. They are takers
you see, like leeches, they latch on and suck you dry. They have been trying to latch
onto me for years. Sometimes one or two of them gets to me, but until recently I was
able to keep them away. I bottled them up and tried to keep them from coming for you
girls, but I fear I may have been wrong in keeping this from you.

Contained in this letter is a golden locket. One my mother gave to me, and her mother
gave to her. I was told to pass it to you, Cosmina and I am sorry that I did not do so
earlier. I can only explain myself by saying I was trying to protect you. I thought if I
kept the locket from you that they would not follow, that you would be safe. Last night,
before I wrote this, my mother came to me in a dream, she told me what you have been
keeping from me and why you have felt the need to run for all these years. I am sorry

I wasn't there, and I am not there now. The locket is the cage used to bottle them up.
Inside of it are three folded photos that must stay inside, Cosmina, you and Shelly must
find your own photos to place inside as well. This will slow them, starve them, and stop
them from finding you. You must keep the locket hidden, somewhere where it is never too far, and most importantly, you must pass this down to future generations. I kept it because
I thought it would break this cycle of being haunted and living in fear of the shadows,
my actions only put you in more danger. I am sorry.
I love you both so much,
Your mother and grandma, Andreea

Shelly tried to stop the tears from pricking the corners of her eyes while she read, but more than one fell and dotted the page. She read it aloud and as she did the lights of the house flickered. Her parents held hands across the table and with their free hands gripped the sides of Shelly's forearms. When she finished reading she set the letter down on the table face up, as though proving to her parents, and to herself, that what she had just read was what had been written on the page. Her mother loosened her grip on Shelly and her husband and grabbed the locket from where it rested beside the letter. She turned it over in her hands, running her fingers along its edges before carefully handing it to Shelly.

Shelly took it and followed the motions her mother had just performed; turning the locket over in her hands, running her fingers along the edge and the swirling details on its face.

"We need to find the photos, our photos that belong in the locket."

Shelly grabbed the letter again and scanned it quickly, "it doesn't say anything about what kinds of photos we're supposed to use. It could be anything."

"Why don't you open it? See what the other photos look like?"

"Aki, you heard what was in there. She specifically said that the other photos have to stay inside."

"She's right dad. I don't think we can risk taking them out."

Ding Dong. The doorbell rang, followed by a knock at the door. The three of them jumped in their seats and Edward began to let out a low growl. Aki looked nervously at the two women he loved most in his life and told them to stay where they were while he got up to check the door.

He walked over lightly on his toes, careful not to make a sound and even more careful to avoid the windows that lined the right side of the door frame. Pressing his face carefully to the door he peered through the peephole to see Sam standing at the door, raising her hand to knock again. He looked back at them and smiled to let them know everything was all right. Shelly's shoulders relaxed slightly but Cosmina maintained an air of caution, ready to grab Shelly and flee at any moment. As Aki opened the door she grabbed the locket from Shelly and placed it in her pocket.

"Hi," Sam's voice was hollow and cracked as she walked through the door.

The bleached portion of her hair had grown out a noticeable amount and she had lost a significant amount of weight. Her cheekbones were prominent now and her eyes yielded the same dark rings that circled Shelly's. She moved more skittishly now, as though she had an entirely new body that she was unsure of how to use. When Shelly saw her this way she tried to quickly stand, forgetting the condition her own body was in. She winced and slowed her movements, making her way more carefully to Sam. The two embraced and

Cosmina invited Aki to take Edward out for his walk with her to give the girls some privacy.

Sam and Shelly helped each other to the couch where Jibbles was waiting to stretch himself out between the two of them, kneading his claws into their thighs.

Shelly thought of what to say while Sam ran her hand along Jibbles' stomach and scratched at his chin. She opened her mouth to speak but found that the words wouldn't come.

Sam, knowing her question, answered it anyways, "I've been scared. I wish I could say good or bad, or sad even, but I've just been scared. Tom tries to visit me almost every day and I feel like a monster telling my dads to send him away but I can't see him without picturing his body all shredded and grey. In the night I hear the thing in the woods, my dads said they hear it too. The shrieking isn't even the worst part, it's the wails that stop me from leaving my room. It sounds like it's coming from every room in my house like it's surrounding me. And the yipping," she shivered, "it's like my body is in a permanent state of shock. I've wanted to call you so many times, to ask you how Tom is, to see how you and Edward are, but part of me feels like I died back there and none of you are even here anymore," her voice started to tremble and the words caught in her throat.

Shelly didn't know what to say. She just held her friend's hand and tried her best to provide comfort where she knew there was none. Sam was right, it felt like part of them had died that day and when Shelly looked at her, she could see the parts that had.

Chapter 6

an ending

Tom arrived before dark, Cosmina and Aki had come inside and the three friends sat on the couch and told them the true story of what had happened that day out in the woods. Tom told them about his father and how he used to live in the house and confessed to Shelly and Sam that sometimes he still heard the shrieking cries in the forest as well. He seemed ashamed of the last part, as though it was somehow his fault all of this had happened. They assured him it wasn't his fault and Shelly reminded him that he had told her not to go in there and she had gone anyways.

Then Shelly and Cosmina shared their dreams and Cosmina told Shelly about the things she had seen when Shelly was a baby and the worse things she had seen when she was growing up. The darkness that would wrap its talons around her mother's body and leave her sick and in her bed for days at a time. Tom and Sam sat beside each other and she apologized for not seeing him and explained that she had been petrified that whatever had been in the woods would walk through her door if she agreed to see him. Aki made tea and passed mugs around to everyone before lighting the fire that sputtered to life in their fire pit that was due for a cleaning. He stood up suddenly and turned to his daughter.

"Shelly, you said you were dreaming this morning when we woke you up. Why haven't you told us about that one?"

Shelly looked around the room nervously and told him she didn't know. She changed the subject by calling Edward over to her and asking him how he had felt today.

Aki pressed on, "maybe it was important. Don't you think we should talk about it?"

She kicked over her tea, feigning an accidental spill, "shit, do you think you could get me some more tea dad?"

Her mother gave her a weird look and Shelly gave her one back warning her to be quiet.

"Of course Shell," he bent to pick up the mug and told the group he would be right back with tea and a cloth to clean up.

"What was that?" Cosmina whispered it sharply to Shelly, leaning in toward the couch from the chair she had pulled up adjacent to it.

"Has dad ever called me Shell?"

Cosmina thought for a moment then furrowed her bro, "no."

"Exactly, look at him when he comes back. Really look at him."

Sam leaned in to ask what was going on and quickly shot back to try and act as casually as possible when Aki walked back into the room. He brought Shelly her tea and wiped up the mess she had made that was now cool to the touch. As he did so, Cosmina stared at him, squinting her eyes to try and see what Shelly was talking about. Shelly threw her eyes toward his neck in an attempt to steer her mother in the right direction. Cosmina looked again, this time searching her husband's neck and then she saw it, a slight shimmer of darkness. When she saw it seemed to spread until it was covering Aki's entire back, then his head and his arms and his legs. She threw her hand over her mouth to stifle her gasp.

He whistled as he cleaned and then turned to walk back into the kitchen, Cosmina gave him a sweet smile as he did and couldn't bring herself to look away until he had fully disappeared back into the kitchen.

"We need to get these two out of here."

"No," Tom and Sam said in unison.

Then Sam spoke on her own, "I have an idea."

Before they could stop her Sam ran to the kitchen and began speaking in a frantic, panicked tone,"Aki, I need your help. My dad's just called. Something is in the house, they called the cops but they're so far away and I'm so scared. Please, can you go check on them, please?"

Tom looked at Shelly searching her face for any indication of what the fuck was going on.

They heard Aki reluctantly agree before coming back into the living room and telling them not to move or do anything without him, it was safer in numbers he said, and the best thing they could do to stop whatever was happening would be to work together. Then he flew out the door and the next sound they heard was the gravel shooting up from under the car tires as he drove away.

"Okay, what the fuck is going on?"

"They have him, at least one of them does."

"How do you know?"

"I thought I saw something, but I wasn't sure, then he called me Shell. He never calls me that. Mom, you saw it to right?"

Cosmina nodded.

Sam was pacing in the living room, rubbing her temples and trying to avoid Jibbles as he walked in and out of her feet. She stopped just as she was about to trip over him, "the locket. We need to figure out what photos go in that thing, like now."

Cosmina reached into her pocket, then paused and looked at Shelly before panic shot across her face. She dug into another pocket, then another, frantically emptying them one by one.

"Shit, he has it."

Tom shot to his feet and pulled out his phone, already dialling Aki's number.

Shelly looked around the room, at the fear on her mother's face, the frantic desire to help on Tom's, and at the strange lifelessness that had taken over Sam. She grabbed Tom's phone from him as he was about to hit call and tossed it onto the couch.

"No."

"What?"

They all looked at her, panic beginning to rise in them again. She could see her mother searching her for a shadow as well.

"I didn't talk about my dream earlier because something was telling me not to. I don't think we need the locket. Mom, did they ever stop coming when you ran?"

"No, well, for periods yes, they would disappear and then out of nowhere they would come back again."

"And your dreams, they were always of you drowning?"

"Yes, always."

"Was there ever anything different about them? Even one thing out of place?"

She thought for a moment, raking her memories for anything out of the ordinary, even something as small as a stray rock, then she remembered the dream she had when she first discovered she was pregnant.

"Yes actually, when I found out I was pregnant with you. There was this old woman. I had been swept away by the flood that always came and I was trying to pull myself to the surface. The water was crystal clear and I remember thinking that was odd since it was usually so murky. I remember I could see the top of a sort of caravan-like wagon behind her and there was a man in the distance smoking a cigar. I couldn't see what he looked like but I could see the smoke rising up from his mouth. The woman tried to reach for my hand to pull me out of the water but I was too scared to take it. I didn't like that the dream had changed and I let the water pull me away from her. She looked so sad when she pulled away and then I never saw her again."

"The cigar," Shelly contemplated what her mother had said, "mom. Do you remember that old ghost you saw? The cowboy? Did the man with the cigar look anything like him?"

"I'm not sure. I really couldn't see much. He was so far away and the water made everything look strange and blurred

from that distance, but I suppose it could have been him. Why?"

"Well, last night I dreamt of great grandpa Andrei. He told me he saw the shadows too, but not like how we see them or how grandma Andreea and grandma Cecilia saw them. He said that the ones he saw were more like ghosts, like people he knew before he died. Then he said something that I've been trying to understand since I woke up. He said that some of our shadows were like his, and that some of them are his."

Sam had stopped pacing and was now sitting in the chair Aki had pulled up beside Cosmina's.

"What does that mean, some of them are his? And how do we know these dreams actually mean anything?"

Realization flooded over Tom as he said, "deni tsin nadint'i."

Cosmina whipped her head around to him, "what did you just say?"

Shelly came to Tom's defence, "I taught him it. The cowboy said it to me, in my last dream of him. And he - he told me he had spoken to you too - and that you wouldn't listen. Why did you leave those out?"

Shelly felt betrayed by her mother yet again, but this time wasn't like when she found out they were moving, this time there was disappointment burning inside of her with the rage.

"He said you wouldn't listen. That all you wanted to do was run. And you're still running. You're trying to avoid it, to leave it all in the past."

Cosmina tried to reach for Shelly's hands but Shelly pulled them back, "we don't have the locket Shelly, running is the only way out."

Shelly was on her feet now, yelling at her mother as she had at Andrei the night before, "and what then! We just leave dad? Abandon him like we did grandma Andreea?"

Cosmina looked like she had been slapped.

"That's not fair Shelly. I left to give myself a better life away from all of that pain. To give you a better life."

"You left because you were scared."

Now it was Cosmina's turn to yell, "of course I was scared! I've been seeing these things since I was a child! You haven't. They just started to come for you. And you know why? Because I RAN. I ran away because I knew they would want me and they would want you so I left. I'm sorry I didn't listen to the weird man in my dreams but I did what I thought was best."

The room started to darken again and outside the shrieking had begun again, louder than it had ever been. Sam shrunk as small as she could in the chair and shut her eyes as tight as she could. Without hesitation Tom began to run around the house, locking doors and windows, shutting blinds and curtains, anything he could to make the house feel more secure.

"You're not getting it. Running is the problem. You ran, grandma ran, Cecilia and Andrei ran. They ran because they didn't have a choice, grandma didn't have a choice. But we do. We don't have to run anymore. There's probably not even any room left in that locket to try and shove two more pictures in there. It's a very small cell for an exceptionally large amount of awful memories."

Cosmina sunk back into her chair, the look of exhaustion that had suddenly fallen on her was overwhelming.

"What do you mean Shelly?"

Shelly looked at the shadows gripping her mothers arms and wondered why she couldn't see them, wondered if she should say something. Deciding against it, she continued with her explanation, keeping a careful eye on her mother.

"The shadows are an accumulation of everyones ghosts. Everyone before us. Grandma Andreea's were Cecilia's and Cecilia's mothers and Andrei's and probably even further back. Yours and mine are an accumulation of all of those, and I have dads as well. The more we run from them, the stronger they get

because more and more keep piling on top of them. The cowboy from our dreams, he told me grandma Cecilia sent him. I think she sent him to teach me about our family, our traditions. When I met grandpa Andrei there was a village in the distance and I think it was burning. I think he wanted to tell me about it but I wasn't ready. I didn't understand but I think I do now. Mom, I think if we learn about our heritage, our cultures, I think we can make them go away, or at least make them weak enough that they can't hurt us."

"We can't learn the entire cultural history of two completely different cultures that span for centuries in one night Shelly."

Cosmina wanted to have hope but when she tried to think of any possible way that it could work, she didn't see how it could.

"No, you're right, we can't. But we can always start somewhere. Don't you have anything from your parents or your grandparents that they've kept from their traditions? Maybe there's something we can use to start with, something we can use to save dad."

Then there was banging on the door. And Aki was yelling, begging for them to let him in. He sounded panicked but there was something in his voice that made Cosmina stop Tom from opening the door. She shook her head as tears welled in her eyes once more.

"Downstairs," she looked at Shelly, answering her question, she did have one thing.

Tom grabbed Edward as he tried to follow them and carried him down the stairs. Part of him did it for Shelly, but part of him did it for himself. He felt safer with Edward there, even if he couldn't go up and down the stairs by himself.

The four of them rushed into Cosmina and Aki's room. Cosmina double checked the curtains, tucking pillows against the bottoms of them before turning on the light. The banging on the front door grew louder and Aki's yells moved from desperate to wild. Cosmina quickened her pace as she threw open the closet doors and rummaged through a stack of boxes in the back corner. Tucked neatly behind them was the suitcase that Shelly had seen beside the tree in Andrei's camp. It was placed on the bed and Cosmina carefully hit the tabs on either side and they begrudgingly clicked open. She lifted the top and folded it carefully onto the bed. Sam, Tom, and Shelly crowded around it, peering inside and breathing in stale dust. On top of a thick black waist coat with large silver buttons the size of a toonie, and a pair of matching black pants, sat a beautiful wooden box and a red and gold notebook. Shelly opened the notebook and carefully read the inscription sunt cu tine.

"Does anyone know what this means?"

Sam sounded out the words, "sunt soo tine."

Cosmina looked over Shelly's shoulder at the words, "I know that. My mother used to say it to me whenever I would leave after a visit, before Shelly was born, its Romanian. It means, I am with you."

"Wait," Sam looked between Shelly and Cosmina, "Romanian? I thought that Andrei was Romani. Aren't those different things?"

Cosmina took the book from Shelly and read over the inscription again before closing it.

"They are, but my grandfather was born in Romania and that's where his people lived. They spoke a dialect called Vlax Romani but he spoke Romanian as well. And when he moved to Canada it was safer and easier for him to be Romanian than it was for him to be Romani, so that was the language he primarily spoke aside from English. He even chose to write in it, just incase."

"Open the book again, is it all in Romanian?"

Cosmina flipped through the pages, "No, some of it looks like maybe its Vlax, I'm not sure I don't know the language. And some of it's in English."

"Maybe he wrote things he didn't want others to know in Vlax and things he only wanted certain people to know in Romanian?"

It had been so long since Tom had spoke that it made the women jump, and he felt the need to apologize.

Cosmina gripped the book and looked at Shelly, "you still remember that saying the cowboy taught you?"

"Of course."

"Good, I have a plan. I need you all to trust me."

▪

It took some convincing, mainly of Sam, to let Aki back into the house. The second Tom opened the door the anger faded from his face and was replaced by a forced concern for his family. Cosmina rushed up to him and asked if he was okay, pretending to check his body for any possible signs of injury.

He stopped her.

"Why weren't you opening the door?"

She met him with level eyes, careful to not let her emotions betray her.

"We were hiding in the basement, we thought it would be safer there."

The kids stood behind her, nodding in agreement. He looked at them skeptically and tried to move around her to Shelly. She let him, and as he walked past her she wrapped her arms around him, pressing her body into his. He tried to shake her off, throwing his shoulders from side to side but she held firm. Then Shelly grabbed him, and told him how much she loved him, and Cosmina started to do the same. He thrashed wildly and started to back toward the door, hoping to loosen Cosmina's grip by smashing her into it. Then Tom grabbed him and squeezed, and Sam followed. They held him tightly but not in anger.

Coyotes began to howl outside and the sound of claws on glass could be heard from the living room. Edward began to growl and snarl at the door that let out to the patio and Jibbles was hissing wildly at the front door. A loud bang came from the door, then another, followed by the shrieking that soon turned into a wail. Sam let go to cover her ears, her body dropping to the floor. She looked up at Tom whose head was now falling to one side, held on only by a thin layer of quickly tearing skin. Sam screamed and crawled backward as quickly as she could toward the door. Another wail sent her into a panic and she wrapped her arms around her legs, rocking back and forth.

Cosmina could tell they were running out of time and yelled to Shelly, "are you ready?"

"Yes," Shelly yelled back over the wailing and the howls that now surrounded them.

The lights flickered and suddenly they were in darkness. They knew they had to do it now.

"Deni tsin nadint'i," Shelly whispered it to her father.

"Sunt cu tine," Cosmina spoke softly in unison with her daughter.

For a moment nothing happened, the wailing continued, the scratching quickened and became more frantic, and Aki continued his attempts to break free. Then suddenly he stopped.

Tom let go first, then Shelly, then Cosmina, who caught Aki as his legs gave out and he slumped to the ground. She lowered him gently as the power flickered back on and the house was illuminated once more. Shelly ran over to Sam and told her to open her eyes, that Tom was okay and it was just a trick being played on her by the shadows.

▪

They sat once more in the living room, the doors still locked and the curtains still drawn. Cosmina and Shelly took turns explaining to Aki what had happened and how Shelly had figured out how to put an end to all of the terror that was being inflicted on them.

"One thing I don't understand is how Sam and Tom saw that thing in the woods before we even got here."

Sam spoke up now after staying silent for most of the explanation including her plan to send Aki away, which she let Tom explain.

"Tom told me once that he thought the thing in the woods came for lonely people, and I think he was right. And no matter how much you all loved each other, you had all of these ghosts from who knows how many past generations haunting you, and all of that pain would make anyone lonely, so it came for you to."

"So that's it then? They're gone?"

Cosmina shook her head and grabbed her husbands hand that had been trembling since the shadows had let go of him.

"They're not even close to gone. But they will be. We don't know if they will ever fully go away, I don't think all of that pain will ever truly be gone. But what we can do is learn, and reconnect and stop running," she looked at Shelly as she said this, "and if we can do all of that then the shadows don't hold any power over us anymore."

Shelly held up the book she had taken from her great grandfathers suitcase.

"I know just where to start."

She opened it and read the inscription. I am with you.

www.ingramcontent.com/pod-product-compliance
Lightning Source LLC
Chambersburg PA
CBHW070357200726
48294CB00003B/964

* 9 7 8 1 9 9 0 4 9 6 2 3 3 *